LOVE, ME

A CHRISTMAS WISH NOVEL

JACQUIE BIGGAR

WAVEFRONT PUBLISHING

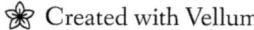

Secrets, Lies & Alibis

I've had the privilege of reading some of the previous books by this fantastic author, and this next installment is a wonderful addition to the series. Not only is this story a fast-paced action-adventure and romance, but it also emphasizes the strength of relationships, such as love and comradery between friends and family. It's a page-turning story and I give it five stars!!

— Tammy- Amazon Reviewer

Perfectly Imperfect

More than just a romantic comedy, "Perfectly Imperfect" is the sprinkled donut in a big old box of regular glazed donuts of rom com fiction.

— Reedsy Reviewer

The Sister Pact

This is a beautiful story about family, siblings, sisters, emotional healing, and true loves. Jacquie Biggar writes with perfection and infuses every story with warmth to touch a reader's heart. The Sister Pact is another perfect gem.

For a special little girl I met via Instagram,

This book is based on the true story of a little girl's life-changing battle with cancer. I met Luna on Instagram and was immediately taken with her warm spirit and positive attitude even though continuous chemo treatments are ravaging her body. She works hard to stay strong and her beautiful smile is never very far away. If you get the chance, follow her. She's an inspiration!

https://www.instagram.com/luna_perrone/

"Christmas is the day that holds all time together."

— ALEXANDER SMITH

INTRODUCTION

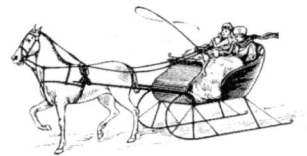

Will a Christmas wish bring two lonely hearts together and give a little girl the family she's always wanted?

Single parent, Grace Donovan arrives in the small town of Emerson with the hope a trial program at the local cancer clinic will be the answer to prolonging her young daughter's life. She doesn't expect to fall for her handsome boss.

As principal of Emerson Elementary, Kyle Roberts is aware of the students' medical issues and his heart goes out to little Cassie Donovan and her mother. When he learns Grace needs a job, he fabricates a childcare program, and is pleasantly surprised by its success. Now, if only he could help Cassie's recovery and get Grace to give him a chance before she learns of his duplicity.

Cassie Donovan barely remembers the father who died when she was just a toddler, but she does know her mother is sad. Even though Cassie wants a puppy more than anything, she gives up her wish to ask for a daddy from Santa Claus, that way if she gets sick again, Mommy won't be alone.

This Christmas, two families are brought together by a Christmas wish and a child's need for a miracle.

3

Grace sipped her coffee and tried to recover her composure. Kyle Roberts was not what she'd expected of an elementary school principal. He was nothing like kindly Mr. Buckle, her first experience with school leaders. Where Mr. Buckle had gray sideburns and pristine suits, Mr. Roberts wore jeans and a white shirt rolled up at the cuffs. Short, dark hair framed a face filled with interesting planes and angles, dark eyes, and a five o'clock stubble that begged to be touched. But it was his captivating smile that set her pulse racing.

"So, Grace, how do you like Emerson? I believe I read in Cassie's file you had recently moved here?" Kyle held a plate with a mini cake topped with chocolate cream icing out to her and shrugged good-naturedly when she shook her head. "Your loss. Mrs.

Fredericks owns the bakery in town and usually sells out by one."

"I try to avoid sweets," she murmured, stifling the urge to lick the chocolate from his lips. "You, umm, have icing... here." She touched her bottom lip for example.

His gaze darkened as male interest ignited. He used a napkin to remove the frosting and cleared his throat. "Better?"

Cleaner—she wouldn't say better. She nodded and hurried to change the subject. "Emerson seems nice, though it's proving somewhat difficult to find a job." *Way to go. Discussing finances as a mood killer —psych 101.*

He smiled and moved aside as a young couple strolled up with the cutest little baby in a stroller. "Keith, Rachel, glad you could make it today."

"Are you kidding?" Keith said, nodding toward a towheaded boy holding a black and white bunny in one of the pens. "We've heard about this shindig for two weeks now. Thomas saved his allowance so he could get a new pet—and it looks like he's made his choice."

Rachel grimaced. "A rabbit, Keith? Is that a good idea?" She reached down and plucked the fussing baby from the buggy. "What about Toby?"

"If it helps, bunnies are fairly easy to train. They'll

even use a litterbox." Grace immediately regretted offering advice as three pairs of eyes pinned her to the floor.

"Well, that's reassuring," Keith said with a warm smile. "Are you Kyle's new... friend?"

Kyle chuckled. "Subtle, buddy, real subtle." He turned to Grace. "Ignore this ne'er-do-well, he's my brother."

Grace hoped her hot cheeks went unnoticed as she smiled at the now contented infant. "How old?"

Rachel kissed the downy cheek and lifted the child against her shoulder. "He's three months—Tobias, after my father." She gently patted the tiny back. "Do you have children, Miss...?"

"Donovan, and its Ms. but please, call me Grace." Aware they were drawing a small crowd, she nodded toward the pet enclosures. "My daughter is over there, she bugged me to come today, as well." Grace raised her brow at Kyle. "Good marketing strategy there, Principal Roberts."

He grinned good-naturedly and shrugged. "It was just a few flyers. Who knew so many kids would be interested in an animal fostering event?"

Rachel gave him the look. "Hope you're available for pet care duties, Uncle Kyle."

He raised his hand and sputtered. "Whoa, there.

It's not my fault you pay your kid such a big allowance. I'd rethink that one if I were you."

"I think Avery needs a goat. Let's go help her pick one out, Rach," Keith said, turning the stroller around. "Nice to meet you, Grace. Don't let this guy talk you into anything—he's a born salesman."

"No to the goat, and I'll take that as a compliment, thanks. See you at dinner?" Kyle called as his family wandered away. Keith raised his hand without turning and they soon disappeared in the rainbow swirl of raincoats and gumboots filling the auditorium.

"They seem nice," Grace murmured, feeling the loss of David. Her husband had been a tease, as well. She wished... well, it didn't matter. This was the real world and she needed to put the past to rest and move on.

"Keith's a good guy. He and Rachel were childhood sweethearts—there's never been anyone else for him." Kyle set his cup in the dirty dish bin. "About that job, were you serious?"

Grace stared at him, speechless. Could the answer to her prayers be Principal Roberts? A moment later, Cassie and Avery ran up, faces glowing.

"Mom, come see the puppies—they're so cute." Cassie tugged on Grace's hand, awakening her from her stupor.

"Yeah, Dad. There's one with curly brown fur.

Hurry, before someone else gets him." Avery grabbed her dad's hand and pulled.

Grace sighed. Maybe it was a blessing in disguise. Kyle Roberts was a distraction. Whatever he had been about to offer, she wasn't sure she should accept. Then again, it would be silly to let her pride stop her from what could be the position she'd been looking for.

His brow quirked, as though he knew what she was thinking. "Are you willing to hear me out?"

Why was she hesitating? She needed the work and he was offering a possible solution. She should hug the man. Figuratively, of course.

"Yes, I'm interested. As long as it doesn't include pet sitting, that is," she said, referring back to his sister-in-law's warning.

He chuckled and allowed himself to be pulled toward the crowded puppy pen. "You've got a deal. Join us for dinner this evening and I'll go over the details."

Dinner? Like a date? No, of course not. His family would be there. Which made no sense. Was he going to offer her a job in front of them? Just as she thought, bad idea.

"I can't. I have no one to watch Cassie. Maybe, you could email me the details?" Then she could think it over in private.

They were at the enclosure now. There had to be

twenty dogs of every breed and description. Cute little basset hounds, roly-poly mixed breeds, labs and shepherds, but it was the quiet Cocker Spaniel pup in the corner that took Cassie's eye. She entered the pen and waded through the animals until she could kneel beside the brown and white dog, its ears wavy and impossibly soft. Avery's choice was a mixed breed, maybe poodle cross, with a playful personality. It kept jumping at the other pups' heads, sending them rolling in a spirited tussle.

"Looks as though Christmas is coming early to Emerson," a bemused parent said as they watched their children fall for the four-legged creatures.

Just what Grace needed. She could barely take care of the two of them already. What was she going to do with a dog?

"So, dinner? You're welcome to bring your daughter. She and Avery can decide names for their mutts." Kyle smiled. "Kidding. I'm not trying to guilt you into fostering a dog, though it is for a good cause." He winked.

Grace's lips turned up in a reluctant grin. "I see what your brother meant. Dinner, yes, thank you. The hound, I'll have to think about." But as she watched Cassie cuddle the pup, she had a feeling the decision had been taken out of her hands.

4

Grace pulled up in front of a quaint two-story Craftsman-style bungalow and turned off her aging SUV. A light drizzle blurred the dancing lights adorning the eaves and the sparkling Christmas tree in the window, but it couldn't detract from the giant red sleigh sitting in the front yard.

"Is this Avery's house?" Cassie whispered, her nose pressed to the glass.

"I believe so," Grace said, double-checking her phone's navigation system. She rubbed her hands nervously up and down the dark slacks she'd chosen to wear with a cranberry blouse. Maybe they should run home so she could change—or better yet, call with an excuse why they couldn't make it—but then the door opened, and it was too late.

Kyle stepped out on the deck and squinted at

their vehicle as though making up his mind whether it was his company or a towaway. Grace couldn't blame him. Her old Betsy might be reliable, but pretty she wasn't.

"I guess that's our cue. Are you ready?" She lifted the casserole dish of bread pudding she'd brought as a contribution to the meal and slid out of the car, shivering as the cold rain pelted her skin. "Pull up your hood," she reminded Cassie, who tended to get sick at the drop of a hat. With the holidays around the corner, it would be nice if they could take part in some of the local festivities this year.

"Do you think Principal Roberts knows Santa Claus?" Cassie asked, hopping down from the vehicle to stare wide-eyed at the sleigh.

"I guess you'll have to ask him." Grace rounded the front of the SUV, wishing she'd remembered the umbrella. "Hurry now, before you get soaked to the skin."

Cassie gave the sled one last glance then ran up the steps and stopped short when she noticed Kyle.

"Hello, Cassie. Do you like my new lawn ornament?" he asked and lifted his gaze to smile as Grace climbed the stairs. "I wasn't sure you'd come."

She cradled the casserole dish and warned her heart to quit pitter-pattering at the sight of a charismatic smile. "You made the invitation too tempting to ignore." She held out the dessert she'd made. "This is for you—bread pudding."

He lifted an eyebrow and accepted the gift. "Where have you been all my life? Desserts are one of my weaknesses." He grinned and ushered them into the house. "Come in, the others are in the den."

Grace took Cassie's hand and followed Kyle into a brightly lit foyer, her skin hot at the touch of his hand on her back.

"Is Santa here?" Cassie asked, providing a welcome distraction.

Kyle looked surprised, then he chuckled. "Oh, you mean because of the sleigh?"

Cassie nodded her head solemnly. "I want to ask him if he got my letter."

Grace crouched to undo her shiny pink coat. "Honey, Santa's elves help him read the lists or he'd never get through all of them."

"Your mom is right, but Santa Claus still has the final say on every gift," Kyle said just as Avery skipped into the room. "That's why it's so important to be good all year, right Miss Mouse?"

Avery rolled her eyes. "Daddy, you *always* say that. Hi, Cassie," she chirped.

Cassie lifted her hand. "Hi."

"Why are you standing out here?" Avery asked, dancing in place.

Grace wished she had half her energy. "We were just asking your dad about the sleigh outside. Cassie thought maybe Santa Claus was coming to dinner, as well." She smiled gently to let her daughter know she was teasing.

Avery laughed. "That's silly. He's busy at the North Pole."

"Avery be nice," Kyle admonished. He took Cassie's coat and hung it on a peg by the door, then did the same for Grace. "The sleigh is one I built. You never know when Santa's might break down. We wouldn't want him to miss delivering any kid's presents, now would we?" He grinned.

Grace was beginning to see what made him a good principal. He was firm, but kind, too. She was relieved to know Cassie would be in good hands at the school. It had been a tough decision making the move after the start of a school year, but there was a new program available for kids like Cassie, and Emerson was one of the first to implement it into their hospital—she had to try.

"C'mon, Cassie, I'll show you my room. I have a unicorn bedspread." Avery grasped her hand and tugged.

When she hesitated, Grace gave a reassuring smile and the girls raced away leaving her alone in the narrow entry with Kyle. Uncomfortable, she patted down her damp hair, aware of its propensity to curl after a rain shower.

"You look lovely tonight," Kyle murmured, his gaze on her face.

"Thank you." She flushed, unused to receiving compliments. Her life the last few years had been focused on her daughter's care and staying ahead of the bills. There wasn't much time for a personal life—or men who looked like Kyle Roberts.

Laughter from another room jerked her gaze down an ambient-lit hallway running beside a dark wood staircase that led to the second floor. Her pulse fluttered. Meeting new people always stressed her out and this time seemed even harder, the stakes higher somehow.

"It sounds as if you have a houseful," she said nervously.

He chuckled, relaxed and handsome. "You know how it goes, you invite two people and they invite two, and so on. Don't worry, they won't bite. Everyone is curious, that's all."

No pressure then.

"I'm boring, trust me. Single mother looking for job—I'm a walking cliché." Her joke fell flat and his smile dropped away. "Look, maybe tonight isn't a good idea. If you could call Cassie, we'll get out of your hair and let you return to your guests." She wasn't up to being the entertainment for his little soirée.

"Grace, slow down." He set the casserole dish on a side table and reached out to grasp her hands. "We're all friends here—well, except for Keith, I *had* to invite him." He grinned, inviting her to share the joke. "Would it help if I explain the position I had in mind before we go in?"

So much. She needed a job, but his mysterious way of telling her anything made her wonder just what he had in mind.

"I'm not going to become your escort," she warned, jerking her hands free. Though to look at him it wasn't likely he needed to pay for female companionship. And now she was just making a fool of herself. *Great.*

Instead of throwing her out of his home, as he had every right to do, Kyle tilted his head, a dark lock of hair falling over his brow, and eyed her consideringly. "Well, that's more interesting than what I was going to offer," he murmured.

Man, just kill me now.

KYLE FOUGHT the grin flirting with his lips. Grace Donovan was proving to be full of surprises. It didn't hurt that she was eye-catching with her lustrous honey-blond hair and emerald green eyes that flashed when she was agitated—like now.

Even though they'd just met, she had been on his mind all day. He wasn't usually so invested in his students' personal lives, but after learning of Cassie's health issues he'd been filled with compassion for the child and empathy for the parent trying to go it alone under such trying circumstances. He wanted to help.

And then he'd met Grace and his heart hitched.

When he'd seen her in the entry to the gymnasium with the harsh overhead lighting playing over her too-thin face and defiant chin, he'd known she was someone he had to meet. Fate or kismet, call it what you will, Kyle believed in it. How else to explain his participation in today's event when he had a hundred and one other things he should be attending to, and the sixth sense that had him glancing at the entrance just as Grace arrived. He'd been drawn to her side like a lodestone and hadn't wanted to let her out of his sight since then. Hence the brilliant job idea he'd come up with on the fly. Now he just had to sell it to her.

"I'm sorry," she said, her cheeks scarlet. "I have a bad habit of talking before I think, it's embarrassing."

If her daughter hadn't been upstairs with Avery, he was quite sure she would have slipped through the door and disappeared into the night. Instead, she straightened her shoulders and faced him, even if her gaze was somewhere north of his face.

She cleared her throat. "If the opportunity is still available, I'd very much like to hear about it—thank you."

So polite. He preferred a woman who spoke her mind, it was... refreshing. "It's more of a transitional post, something to help me and hopefully give you room to breathe until the right job comes along." He gestured to a deacon's bench along one wall and waited until she took a seat before he sat next to her—leaving plenty of space between them. "So," he started, suddenly nervous. "Without knowing your background, I took a guess from seeing how you interacted with the children today that you're comfortable with them, yes?"

She raised a brow. "I have a daughter, remember?"

"Okay, maybe I didn't word that correctly," he admitted, chuckling. "What I mean is, are you comfortable caring for a group of kids for a few hours before, and after, school?"

Grace's head tipped and her hair caressed her shoulder—lucky hair.

"Like babysitting?" she asked, her tone dubious.

He smiled. "Childcare, yes. Many of our students come from families where both parents work. This can create a conflict for getting their children to school on time and picked up afterward. My plan is to do a month-long trial leading up to Christmas. I'll have a notice sent inviting parents in need to bring their children to the library an hour or two before school starts for a nominal fee. If it goes well, we can revisit the project in the new year and cement a proposal for the school board." He tried to gauge what she was thinking, but her normally expressive eyes were shuttered.

She stood and paced to the door before whirling around, anger radiating from her pores. "When did you come up with this *brilliant* idea?" she snapped.

He stared at her, bemused. She really was magnificent. Unfortunately, her near-screech brought Keith, Rachel, and the rest of his guests streaming down the hallway.

"What did you do now?" Keith joked, glancing from Kyle to Grace.

Kyle stood, annoyed at the disruption. "It's a misunderstanding. Can you give us a moment, please?" He gave his brother a meaningful look. "I think the roast is burning."

Keith hesitated, then turned to herd everyone into the kitchen. "Quick, we have to save dinner."

When they were gone, Kyle risked the few steps to move closer to Grace, hoping her bark was worse than her bite. "I know what you're thinking but you're wrong. The idea for childcare at the school has been on my mind for some time now. We have many parents like you, single mothers and fathers who struggle to do the best they can for their kids. I want to help them."

He put his hand on the wall near her head and leaned in for emphasis. "It's true, after you mentioned you were looking for work and I saw you interacting with the children today, I jumped into action—but anyone who knows me will tell you I'm impulsive. I didn't mean to embarrass you in any way." He got lost in her turbulent eyes. "Do you forgive me?"

She sighed and her breath brushed his cheek, sending goosebumps tripping over themselves as they raced down his spine.

"I don't have a choice, do I? When do you want me to start?"

5

The waiting room was quiet in the small clinic of the Emerson Hospital. Too quiet. It gave Grace time to second-guess her decision to enroll Cassie in a clinical trial even though Dr. Simons, the oncologist, had assured her this was her daughter's best chance for a full recovery.

She picked up one of the glossy magazines scattered across the table separating her from another distraught couple, then tossed it back with barely a glance at the cover. The woman's worn eyes met hers before she went back to comforting her wife with an arm around her shoulders and interlocked hands.

Grace wanted to assure them they were doing the right thing, but she wasn't so sure she believed it herself. Cassie was doing well. Why mess with her treatment on a maybe?

Because she wanted/needed her daughter to survive.

The answer hung in the air, filling the space with hope and trepidation in equal measure. She'd been over the paperwork a thousand times. COG limited institution trials went through a vigorous process before they were approved for children. Her baby would be as safe as possible, given the circumstances.

Leukemia.

Every person's worst nightmare, never mind when the disease is attacking your precious child.

"Mrs. Donovan?" A kind-looking nurse in pale blue scrubs stood near an open door, thick folder in hand.

Stomach plunging, Grace rose and followed the woman into an office with dark paneled walls, a tidy desk with a large desktop computer, and tufted leather chairs.

"Have a seat, the doctor will be with you shortly." The nurse set the paperwork squarely in the center of the desk, tapped a few keys on the keyboard, then left the room, softly closing the door behind her.

Grace twisted bloodless fingers in her lap and bit her bottom lip. Her baby was barely six years old and had a file thicker than Grace's wrist. It broke her heart to see it laid out like that, months of tests, chemotherapy, and hospital rooms. Through it all, Cassie had maintained her sweet smile. She was such a good kid who deserved so much more than the hand she'd been dealt. Which is why they were here, she had to remember that. If there was the slightest chance...

The door opened and a handsome man in a suit and tie entered. He nodded at Grace, who gripped her purse strap, and circled his desk to face her across its width. Sitting, he loosened his tie and opened the folder to peruse the contents.

"So, Mrs. Donovan, I understand you are interested in joining our Children's Oncology Group trial, is this correct?"

"It's Ms. Donovan. My husband passed away three years ago. Cassie's oncologist recommended you as her best chance of a full recovery. That's a tall order, Doctor. Can you back it up?" If he couldn't instill some confidence within the next few minutes, she would take Cassie and go back home so she could be near her grandparents and friends.

He steepled his fingers under his chin and gazed at her with somber gray eyes. "I think we started out on the wrong foot." He held out his hand, gold watch gleaming on his wrist. "David Michaels. I know you have concerns and I'm happy to answer them the best that I can, but I'd be lying if I said your daughter is guaranteed to come out of this cancer-free.

"What I can say, is that we will do everything we

can to make sure her prognosis is as positive as we can make it. The treatment will last from two to three years with a lifetime of follow up studies, which should give you some peace of mind. Your daughter will be well taken care of, Ms. Donovan, I give you my word."

"It's Grace," she said absently. "Can you explain these trials? I've heard that some groups are given placebos. If that's true, I want Cassie out. She's not a guinea pig."

He gave her a faint smile and closed the folder before leaning back in his chair. "There are no placebos. Our patients receive medications based on their health and the trial they are involved in. Your daughter would be part of our phase III group where our studies will test current best options for care against alternatives that promise better cure rates, decreased side effects, or late effects of the treatment. We call these study arms."

"And how will you determine which 'arm' Cassie will be a part of?" Grace was doubtful already and they hadn't even begun. On the one hand, the current best option sounded the safest, but the other options tempted with their higher cure rates and fewer after-effects. She hated to see Cass lying in those hospital beds barely able to lift her head, her skin pale and eyes sunken.

"We don't know how a child will fare until all the

children have completed treatment and been studied for years after, so to be fair, we choose randomly one of the trials. But rest assured, if one treatment is found to work better than the others, all the children are transferred to that program. Your daughter will get the best care available."

"Yes, so you say." Grace frowned at the thick folder on his desk and wished with all her heart she could take the coming months on herself, but she couldn't. All she could do was pray she was making the right decision for Cassie. "And the costs? Are there grants for this sort of thing?" She'd already sold their house and belongings to cover hospital bills, there wasn't much left.

Dr. Michaels hesitated, then gave a slow nod. "Generally, the fees are split between the patient and the state—"

"I'm sorry to have taken up your time, but..." Grace rose, her voice thick with tears.

"But..." Dr. Michaels repeated. "In this instance, the fees have been covered by an anonymous benefactor, so it is not an issue."

A benefactor. For the first time in a long time, she didn't feel so alone. Someone had guided her to this office on this day and now because of the kindness of a stranger, her daughter had a chance of a full recovery. "Let's get started, then."

CASSIE LOOKED up from the doll she'd been trying to dress in an emerald gown for the tea party Avery was planning. Her new friend had just finished dressing her doll and was working on a ponytail for its long, blonde, hair. A three-story white and pink dollhouse took up the wall next to her princess bed and was filled with miniature-sized furniture Cassie eyed enviously.

"Is your daddy coming to the party?" she asked. Avery's dad seemed really nice for a principal.

"Maybe later. He has some stuff to do first." Avery held her fashionable doll up and twisted her this way and that. "What do you think?"

"She looks like my mom."

Avery grinned. "She can have tea with us even if she's not here, see?"

Cassie smiled though her stomach clenched. Mommy had a meeting with their new doctor and asked Mr. Roberts if he would mind watching her for an hour or two. Cass usually attended these consultations with her mom and didn't know what to make of this turn of events. She wanted to tell Avery about her hospital stays, but it was nice to be treated like a regular kid, so she kept quiet. Back home, everyone acted different after they heard what happened—it made her sad. This place was their new start, that's what Mommy said.

Cassie crossed her fingers behind her back.

Avery's eyes lit up. "Hey, what if your mom and my dad become boyfriend and girlfriend?" She giggled and covered her mouth. "We could be sisters."

Sisters.

Cassie looked down at her doll, afraid to even acknowledge the hope ballooning in her chest. If Avery did become her sister, then Mommy wouldn't be alone if she got sick again and couldn't come home. She wished that she had asked Santa Claus for a sister instead of a puppy.

"Has your mommy been gone very long?" Maybe she shouldn't ask things like that, but Avery seemed so happy all the time...

"She's not gone the way you're thinking," Avery said, pointing to a picture on her dresser. A pretty, dark-haired woman smiled at them with her arm around a much younger Avery. "Mom didn't like being married, so she and Daddy 'vorced and she moved to Hollywood to become a famous actress! That's where my dollhouse comes from. She sent it for my birthday last year."

Suddenly, Cassie's problems didn't seem so big. Avery pretended it didn't bother her, but the way her shoulders hunched, and her eyes grew sad, Cassie knew that it did. Imagine, not having your mom show up for your birthday!

Determined to cheer her friend up, Cassie leaned forward and whispered, "Guess what I asked Santa for?"

Avery straightened, curiosity drawing her near. "What?" she whispered back.

"You can't tell, or it won't come true," Cassie warned, her heart thrumming like a frightened bird.

"I won't. Promise." Avery held a bent finger out. "Pinky swears."

Twining her finger with the other girl's, Cassie squeezed and at the last minute went with the easier answer. "A puppy." Her dream of a new father was too personal to share just yet.

Avery clapped her hands together, startling Cassie. "I did, too. I can't believe we asked for the same gift— it's fate."

Teamed up with the animal fair they'd attended, it certainly seemed like it, but Cassie had learned the hard way not to wish for miracles, so she just smiled.

The doorbell rang and her stomach plunged. Mom was back and now she'd have to leave.

"Let's sneak out and listen by the stairs. Maybe you can stay for a while." Avery put a finger to her lips and led the way to the spindled banister. "Shh," she whispered as her dad came into view and opened the door.

"That was fast," he said, stepping back to allow Mommy into the entry.

Cassie grasped the posts and stared at the top of their heads, her breath coming in little pants she tried to control. She wanted to hear how the meeting went, but the thought of another round of medicines and the accompanying sickness scared her. She was feeling good now, couldn't they wait? Maybe the cancer was gone.

Her mind filled with worrying thoughts, it took a minute to hear what was being said downstairs.

"You seem upset," Mr. Roberts said.

Mommy shook her head. "Just tired. It's been a busy few weeks. By the way, I've thought over your proposal, and if the position is still available, I accept."

Avery's dad closed the door and turned, glancing up the staircase. The girls leaped back, skidding on their bums, and covering their mouths to muffle the nervous giggles threatening to give them away.

"That was close," Avery mouthed.

"Let's go back to your room," Cassie whispered, uncomfortable with snooping on their parents' conversation.

Avery looked disappointed but shrugged and frog-hopped the few feet to her bedroom. "It sounds like your mom is going to work at the school, isn't that cool?"

Cassie wasn't so sure. With her mom at the school all day, she'd have to be extra careful. Sometimes her energy was low, especially on gym day. She didn't want her mom coddling her in front of the other kids. It was hard enough to fit into a new class, without having her mom breathing over her shoulder.

"I guess," she mumbled, scuffing her toes in the pink carpet.

Avery peered up at her from her crouched position. "Geez, you don't sound very excited."

Cass flushed. She was right. Instead of being happy her mom had a job, and they could stay in Emerson, she was acting like a big baby. Besides, this way Mommy would be spending more time with Mr. Roberts. Maybe Santa had a plan.

Feeling better, she smiled and pointed to the peach juice they were pretending was tea in the little plastic cups. "Let's celebrate."

Avery's easy-going smile returned. "Yay! I'll pour."

Cassie dropped to the carpet next to the table, forgoing the delicate white chair, and helped herself to one of the mini donuts stacked on a tray. The cinnamon sugar burst on her tongue and coated her lips. Laughing, she licked them off and for the first time in a long time, let go of her worries and had fun.

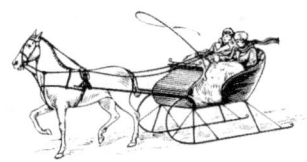

6

Kyle closed the door after Grace and glanced up the stairs in time to catch two curious faces peeking down through the banister rails. Avery's muffled giggles as the girls sneaked back to her bedroom, brought a reluctant smile to his lips. She really was reprehensible, but it was tough to be too strict with her. She'd been through a rough time since her mother's departure for the bright lights, following her dreams—without her family.

"I can't stay for long," Grace said, huddled into her thin coat. "Tomorrow is a school day and I still have laundry to get done."

Straightforward, that was Grace Donovan. What you see is what you get. Between the subtexts his ex-wife had enjoyed using like a knife to the gullet, and the coy simpering of his sometimes date, Tammy, it was refreshing to know where he stood with Cassie's mesmerizing mother.

"I just made hot chocolate for the girls. Can I talk you into a cup?" He moved forward and held out a hand for her jacket. "Looks like you could use something to warm up. Not used to our *wet* coast winters yet?"

Grace cracked a smile at his deliberate slip. "You could say that."

Peeling the damp coat off her shoulders, he sucked in a sharp breath. "You're frozen."

She tucked rain-darkened hair behind her ear and shivered. "It's mostly nerves. The meeting I attended was more stressful than expected."

Kyle pulled his distracted attention from the delicate nape of her neck to the worry lines between her brows and frowned. "Cassie?"

She startled and glanced up the stairs, before meeting his gaze. "Why would you say that?"

Because he didn't like the fear darkening her beautiful green eyes. Guiding her into the spacious kitchen, Kyle strode to the cupboard next to the gas range and took down two mismatched mugs from the colorful assortment he and Avery collected from garage sales and thrift store finds. He stirred the fragrant chocolate mixture in a pot on the stove and filled first one then the other mug, topped them with whipped cream from the fridge and a sprinkle of cinnamon, before carrying the cups to the island where Grace had settled on one of the tall barstools.

"Try it, my mom's secret recipe." He waited until she lifted her drink before taking a sip himself, breathing in the aromatic cinnamon and cocoa with pleasure. "When one of us kids came home with the weight of the world on our shoulders, this was her go-to remedy. Worked every time, too."

"Your mom sounds like a wise lady," Grace murmured. Her lips were covered in whipped cream she attempted to lick with her tongue. Kyle stared, mesmerized, his gut tightening with every swipe. She looked up, caught his intent gaze, and stilled. "That bad?"

Incredibly good, actually. Aware she wasn't ready to hear about his inopportune attraction, he smiled and reached for a napkin from a drawer behind him. "I forgot to warn you they're messy."

She carefully dabbed at her mouth, then folded the napkin into a precise little triangle. "I suppose I should have known you would be apprised of a student's health issues, but I wish you would have said something sooner. Is that why you offered me the childcare position?"

Her gaze warned Kyle to tread lightly. This woman had been through a series of traumatic events that would have crippled anyone else. Yet she sat in his kitchen, a cup of hot chocolate between her hands, and pride shooting from her eyes.

"I offered you the job because the school needs you, no more, no less." He smiled. "Don't worry, you'll earn your wage. Our students are an energetic bunch."

Grace frowned. "I appreciate the offer, I do, but..."

Kyle was losing her and suddenly it seemed incredibly important she stay.

He tapped his fingers on the counter and tried to figure out how much to reveal. "As principal, it's my job to make sure my students thrive at school and go home safe each night. For that reason, it's necessary to know when they may need extra attention or a watchful eye."

He reached out and gently pried one of Grace's hands from her mug. "I would never divulge any child's information to just anyone. The school nurse knows of Cassie's condition and no one else, Grace. I promise. And you, of course, which is another good reason for you to quit giving me grief over this job and just accept it's where you are meant to be." He gave her fingers a brief squeeze and let them go. "So, now can we talk about more important matters? Like when you're going to bake some of those amazing cookies your daughter swears are *the best in the whole wide world?*"

"I'll bring cookies for the staff tomorrow. I assume you'd like me to begin as soon as possible?"

Now that he'd won that round, Kyle relaxed and settled back to enjoy his hot chocolate—and the opportunity to converse with a beautiful woman. "Seven a.m. too early? I'll send out a group email to the teachers this afternoon and they can get in touch with the parents. You may not have too many kids to begin with, but once word gets out, I'm expecting an influx of little bodies to keep you busy."

"Are you planning to segregate according to age group, or...?"

Good question, he hadn't thought that far in advance. With the school covering kindergarten to grade six, it might be difficult to entertain them as a unit.

"We'll start as one and see how it works, then we—by that, I mean you—can diversify as needed. I'll try to get you some assistance as the program gets underway, but no guarantees. I have to prove this is a viable option for afterschool care with the board before they'll open their wallets." Kyle pulled a sheet of paper and a pen from the drawer and wrote out a temporary calendar for Grace.

"So, we'll go with seven to nine Monday to Friday, and three to six except for Thursdays. The library is booked for science fairs on that day."

Grace nodded but a crease furrowed her brow. "You should probably know Cassie will be starting a test program at the hospital in the next few weeks. If they call her to go during these hours, I won't be able to watch the children. You're going to need a backup nanny."

He wanted to ask her thoughts on the program and her daughter's prognosis but didn't want to scare her off by prying. In time, when she was ready, maybe Grace would trust him enough to share her burden. For now, he would do what he could to ease the way for this brave woman.

He stood and struck a comical pose. "Just call me Mrs. Doubtfire."

7

M onday morning's alarm shrilled in Grace's ear. She rolled over to shut it off, then groaned and drew the pillow over her face. What was she thinking? She wasn't trained to care for a room full of noisy little gremlins. She was a photographer, or at least she had been before...

Her husband would tell her she could do whatever she put her mind to, and she'd believed him, until he up and died leaving her to flounder. After Cassie came down sick, she had to pick herself up and cope for her daughter's sake when a dark cave would have suited her better.

Cassie had been so brave, coping with the loss of her daddy and months of cancer treatments. Weak from fevers and low platelet counts that delayed her chemotherapy, she still found a way to face each day with a smile. Grace had been the one to cry when her girl's beautiful blonde curls fell out and she'd railed against a God who would allow this to happen to her child.

But, somehow, they'd managed day by day, minute by minute, until the cancer cells were beaten back and hopeless became hopeful. And now they were here, on the cusp of a trial program that could give Cass, and children like her, the chance of a better life. Whoever their nameless benefactor was, Grace would be forever grateful. There's no way she could have managed the costs on her own.

Her bedroom door creaked open, and Cassie peeked in, her baby fine hair standing on end. "Wake up, Mommy. It's school time."

Grace smiled and patted the bed. "Come and tell me what Miss Sleepyhead is doing up so early."

Cass giggled and streaked across the green shag carpet, the bunny ears on her slippers bouncing adorably. She climbed up and nestled against Grace's side, warm and soft and faintly smelling of the bubblegum bath soap from the night before.

"Today's our field trip to the post office to send our Santa Claus letters to the North Pole, remember, Mommy?"

She did now. How was she going to fit a puppy into their chaotic lives? Never mind the new daddy!

Seeking a distraction from her tumbled thoughts, she rolled onto her side and raised a clawed hand in the air. "Oh, oh. I think it's time for the tickle monster." She dived for Cassie's tummy amid a screech of laughter and her heart filled with joy. Times like these made all the worry worthwhile.

"Okay, you little monkey. Go get dressed and *wait* until I get downstairs before pouring your cereal. I'm still sweeping up crumbs from the last time you tried on your own."

Cass leaped off the bed and ran to the door—a rare bundle of energy this morning. "Hurry, Mommy. I don't want to be late."

"Yes, ma'am." Grace snapped a salute and grinned, pleased to see her daughter acting like a normal six-year-old. The cancer had taken so much of her childhood away from her that these moments were precious.

One day at a time. The mantra took on extra meaning when you were a caregiver. Every day was a win.

After a rushed shower and a hasty breakfast, Grace pulled into the school parking lot just shy of the appointed time only to see agitated parents with children dangling from their hands, while Kyle—Mr. Roberts—worked to keep the peace.

"Oh, oh. I guess I'm late."

Cassie kicked the back of the seat, even though she'd been warned a hundred times not to. "See, Mommy? I told you."

Grace doused the headlights and turned the tired car off with an extra chug-chug from the engine. "Okay, little miss know-it-all. Sarcasm doesn't become you. Let's go before Mr. Roberts sends out a search party."

Cassie giggled, the reprimand sailing right over her head. "That's silly. He can see us right here."

Unfortunately, true. He was sending her mental mayday messages even now.

"I'm coming. I'm coming. Hold your horses." She opened her door, shot the group a quick wave, and hurried around to Cassie's door.

"Do you have your lunchbox and Santa's letter in your bag?" She reached in to unlock the child restraints and gave her daughter a kiss on a velvety cheek before standing back to let her hop out of the vehicle.

"You asked me that five times. Are you scared to take care of these kids, Mommy? Because you don't have to be—it's easy." Cass stared up at her with a furrowed brow.

Grace's throat clenched. She crouched down and

pulled her girl in for a tender hug. "You're pretty great. Do you know that?"

Cass's short arms tightened around her neck in a mini bear hug, then she grabbed Grace's hand and tugged. "Come on. Let's go and make some new friends."

Even though her feet were dragging, Grace laughed and allowed herself to be pulled up the sidewalk toward the waiting parents—were there more now? She'd never been good at this kind of thing, much happier working on her own, preferably in a quiet zone. Going by the crying toddler in one woman's arms and the boisterous boy yanking on his father's pantleg, she wasn't going to find either option here.

Drawing a deep breath, she put on her friendliest smile and stepped forward, her hand out for a shake. "Good morning, I'm Grace Donovan, the new day-care supervisor. I'm sure we're going to have a fun learning experience."

She hoped.

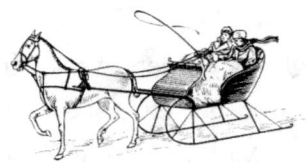

8

Kyle spotted Grace's SUV pulling into the parking lot and blew out a relieved breath. That's what happened without a backup plan. If she hadn't shown, he wasn't sure what he would have done. Actually, that's not true. *He* would have been on child-care duty. Thank goodness it hadn't come to that. He liked kids; he just didn't want to end up on their hit list. Not to mention the school board's. As is, they weren't happy with his impulsive decision to hire a childcare worker just before the holidays and had warned him if anything went wrong it would be on his head. No pressure.

He stood back and let Grace work her magic to placate the irate parents and greet her charges. In a matter of minutes, she had the mothers smiling and the fathers eating out of her delicate hands. The children gazed at her with adoration and the mothers with gratitude, while the few fathers in the group straightened shoulders and puffed paunchy stomachs. He could see why—she looked like an angel under the soft LED lights with her flaxen hair and classic features—but that didn't stop him from the primeval urge to howl at the moon and beat his own pecs to gain her attention. In the end, men were basic creatures in the presence of a beautiful woman.

The rain, never far away during the winter months, fell with a light drizzle which soon turned into a turn-off-the-faucet downpour. The tearful goodbyes were cut short as parents raced for their cars, heads hunched into jacket collars, and the children huddled under an overhang above the door looking like a scraggly bunch of lost sheep.

Kyle nudged his half-asleep daughter leaning against his hip. "Wake up, sweetheart. Time to show Ms. Donovan to the library."

Avery yawned and rubbed her eyes. "I'm tired, Daddy."

He lifted her into his arms, backpack and all, surprised how long her gangly legs had grown. "Just a few more minutes, Peanut. You can rest while I help Ms. Donovan get settled."

"Where's Cassie?" she mumbled into his shoulder.

He hoisted her higher and tugged the heavy ring of keys from the front pocket of his slacks. Jeans were more comfortable, but the school had a strict dress code he would love to see relaxed. One hurdle at a time.

"She's here. See? Good morning, Cassie, Ms. Donovan." He strode past them with a smile and fed the right key into the lock on the first try—go him.

"Hi, Cassie." Avery perked up and waved, her cold fingers clenching the side of Kyle's neck. If he had a camera, he'd capture the moment before his daughter grew too big for his arms, but a mental snapshot would have to do.

The library with its glass paneled exterior walls was to the right, across from the office. Kyle flicked on the lights and stood aside to let the children funnel past. Grace followed, her eyes wide. He was proud of the room, with its aisles of neatly cataloged books. A colorful dragon made of tissue paper undulated over a reading nook made up of toadstools and a playhouse meant to look like a fairy cottage.

Grace turned as the kids dropped their packs and fanned out, some heading to boxes overflowing with building blocks, others to a low table filled with picture books and puzzles. "I'm not sure what I expected, but this is amazing."

Kyle nodded, pleased with her response. "The kids took an active role in decorating. We had an art contest and the winning class from each grade added their projects to the space. I figure that way, they'll take pride in their accomplishment and maybe figure out if you apply yourself, good things happen."

He shifted, uncomfortable under her inquisitive eyes. "What? Have I got toast crumbs on my mouth?"

Grace's gaze flicked to his lips and away, leaving them tingling. She chuckled. "Sorry. You surprise me, that's all. You really enjoy your job, don't you?"

He hadn't to start with. With his business background, Kyle had planned to climb the corporate ranks and prove his in-laws wrong. They had made their displeasure in their only daughter's association with a guy from the *other* side of town clear. His decision to put his career on hold to be closer to Avery only solidified their opinion and ended up destroying his marriage in the end.

"Yeah, I do," he agreed, eyeing the kids using their creativity to shape castles in the sky out of building blocks. He nodded in their direction. "It's hard not to be inspired by the promise I see in their futures. If I can help them reach their full potential in some small way, I'll consider it my reward."

She placed long, slender fingers on his forearm for

a too-brief moment. "You remind me of a teacher I had in fifth grade English class. He always pushed us to do our best—think outside of the box. It wasn't until many years later I realized how much his advice mattered. It's given me the strength to face challenges in my life." She dropped her gaze to his tie, and Kyle's pulse knocked against his chest. "I wonder where he is now?"

He lifted his hand to tuck her hair back so he could catch every fascinating nuance of her expressions, then let it drop as little Sammy Higgins let out a war whoop, his toy car speeding off the end of the table and tumbling onto the imaginary rocks below. "You should look him up some day. I bet he'd love to see how little Grace..."

"Morgan," she supplied, smiling.

He grinned back. "How little Grace Morgan turned out."

She shrugged and started toward Sammy. "Not much to see, I'm just me. I better get to work before you don't have a library left. Maybe I'll see you later?"

Oh, you can count on it.

Aloud, he said, "Coffee room is down the left hall, second last room on the right. I'll send someone in to spare you around nine-fifteen."

She lifted a hand in response and sank to her knees beside a suddenly bashful Sammy, who'd never been shy before. But then, Grace Donovan had that effect on most men.

Whistling under his breath, Kyle left to start his day.

THREE HOURS LATER, his head was pounding, and he was ready to call it a day. At nine a.m.

"I understand," he said, glaring at the intercom on his desk. "But my students have worked hard for this Christmas pageant. We can't cancel it just because of a little heating problem."

The contractor on the other end of the line wasn't having a good morning either, apparently. "It's like I told you, my crew is short three guys and your *little* problem, isn't so little. We have to diagnose the issue, order parts, and remove the existing assembly before we can replace the heater and get you up and running. There's no way that's going to happen in time for the show. You'll have to rebook it for a later date, I'm sorry."

Rebook a Christmas concert until after Christmas? That was like saying there was no Santa Claus.

"I'll figure something out. Just do what you can." Kyle hung up. "Thanks for nothing," he growled and massaged the side of his head where the hammering was the worst.

"Now what?" Keith asked, his voice intruding on Kyle's misery.

"Hell, if I know." Kyle frowned at his brother. "I thought you said those guys could do it, no problem?"

Keith shrugged. "Guess I was wrong. You going to sit there feeling sorry for yourself, or are you going to help me come up with a solution?"

"Help you?" Kyle squawked. "I'm the one about to get thrown under the bus, here."

"Yeah, well... just wait and see. Thomas is playing the innkeeper in his class play and if Rachel doesn't get to video the whole thing because it's *canceled*, where do you think I'll be sleeping for the next month?"

Kyle envisioned his twin in the family's doghouse and a ghost of a smile crossed his lips. "Good thing you built old Jasper a sturdy shack, isn't it?" He leaned back and crossed his arms. "She's right. This *is* your fault. If you'd let me hire someone last spring when that old heater started acting up, we wouldn't be in this position."

Keith shoved his chair and rose, bracing clenched fists on the other side of the desk. "Hey, I did you a favor. After that incident with the flagpole, you weren't in any position to go to the board about an expensive repair like the furnace. I got it going and it probably would have lasted another year or two if someone didn't decide to leave all the doors open after basketball practice." He straightened and flung out his hands. "What were you thinking?"

He hadn't been, obviously. Between the multitude of meetings over Covid-19 protocols now that the virus was contained, the advent of Grace Donovan and her daughter, and the sudden interest his ex-wife was showing in Avery, Kyle could be forgiven for his absentminded blunder. If only it hadn't caused a catastrophe right before Christmas.

"We aren't getting anywhere blaming each another. The question is, what are we going to do now?" Kyle eyed his brother warily.

Keith sagged into the chair and scrubbed a hand through his hair. "Any chance you can book another venue?"

On top of the extra expenditures he'd racked up hiring Grace? Not likely. "I can try. Most halls are already booked for holiday gigs, but you never know, we might get lucky. Thank goodness the school has a separate heater for the gymnasium, or I'd really be screwed."

Just then, his secretary, Carmen, tapped on the door. "Sorry to interrupt, but a student just reported a leak in the boy's washroom."

Kyle's brows furrowed even as his stomach sank. "What sort of leak? Can't the custodian handle it?"

"Mr. Green looked. Apparently, the floor drain is backed up. He thinks you need a plumber."

Kyle exchanged a look with Keith, who shook his head. "Good luck with that."

Kyle was pretty sure luck had packed his bags and vacated Emerson.

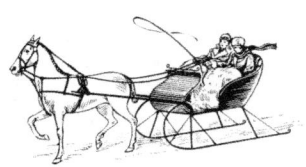

9

Cassie trudged toward the gymnasium, tugging the hem of her shorts over the bandage on her thigh. She'd wanted to wear pants, but Mrs. Samson said gym clothes were a pre... pre... needed if they wanted to participate. And she did. Sports were fun and she wanted fun. She needed fun. Fun stuff made the time in hospital bearable. It gave her something else to think about besides the burns caused by chemo, the constant pain and weakness, and the worry in her mom's eyes.

So, here she was—in shorts.

She plunked down next to Avery on the chilly bleacher and leaned down to tie her sneakers. "Brr, it's cold in here."

Avery rubbed her arms and shivered. "I hope it's

not like this for the play or we'll have to change it to Frosty, the Snowman."

Cassie smiled. Avery always came up with stuff to make her laugh. "Your dad could play Professor Hinkle."

"What happened?" Avery pointed at the sterile compress practically glowing on Cassie's leg.

She slapped a hand over the pad, then winced at the subsequent burst of pain. "It's nothing. Just a scrape."

Thankfully, Avery accepted her explanation and moved on to the next thing that had taken her attention. "Don't look, but Jessica Bigalow is staring at you."

Cassie peeked through her lashes. A girl with hair the color of a brand-new copper penny and a map of freckles covering her cheekbones stood with a trio of other girls. The pointed looks and whispering behind cupped hands made it more than obvious who they were talking about—the new kid.

She faked an uncaring shrug and rose, anxious to join the rest of the class practicing with basketballs in the middle of the gym. "Let's go before all the balls are gone."

"Are you just going to ignore them?" Avery made a grab for—and missed—one of the balls that rolled past and bounced off the nearby wall.

Cassie had better luck. She lifted the orange

sphere, her nose crinkling at the rubbery scent, and started the soothing repetition of dribbling in place.

"Mom says unhappy people are mean 'cause they're hurting inside, and the best thing we can do is to give them the space to work it out."

"Hmm," Avery murmured, snagging her own ball to bounce. "Your mom is pretty smart, isn't she?"

Cassie flicked a quick glance at her friend to see if she was mocking her, but Avery looked serious. "Yeah, she is. That's why..."

A whistle pierced the room. "Class, line up here, please." Mrs. Samson waved a hand toward the center line and crossed her arms to wait.

Jessica and her buddies jogged across the court and spread out, leaving Cassie and Avery no choice but to line up on the other end with the boys.

"Ew, girl germs," a kid chanted, pretending to fall against his buddy, Avery's cousin Thomas.

"Okay, settle down now," Teacher warned and blew the whistle again. "As you may have already guessed, we're going to practice basketball beginning with footwork drills. Starting with Avery, please take a partner from every second student. So, Avery, you'll pair with Curtis, Cassie, you'll be with Thomas, and so on down the line. Grab a ball and separate into your individual groups, then wait for my directions—and no goofing around."

Exchanging a dismayed look with Avery, Cassie hugged the ball to her chest and prayed the class bell would ring. No such luck. Huffing a sigh, she turned to her new partner, only to find him carefully ignoring her as he bounced his ball under the hoop.

He was good at it, too.

Cassie enjoyed sports. At least she had before the chemo sucked all the energy out of her body. How was she going to keep up to Thomas?

"We're going to start with a quick stop drill," Mrs. Samson said. "Set your balls down and face each other but make sure you have room to move." She glanced around the room. "A little further apart, Jessica. That's it, perfect."

She strode to center court. "This is how it's done. Take a step forward, then hop to two feet, adopting a slight crouch over your legs—like so. Pretend your feet are eagle claws. Sink your toes and heels into the floor, bracing your weight on your entire foot. Land soft and stick to the floor. And again," she said, performing the maneuver one more time. "Any questions?" She waited a moment, frowning slightly as a ball rolled across the room as though kicked by ghostly feet, then nodded. "Okay, let's see what you've got." She blew the whistle, and everyone hurried to get into position.

Cassie faced Thomas, her cheeks hot. She was going to make a fool of herself in front of Avery's cousin, she knew it. Why did dumb old Jessica have to be so mean?

"Do you want to go first," he asked, staring at her with deep blue eyes.

She didn't *want* to do it at all, but since he was giving her a choice... "Umm, you can." That way she could watch and learn—hopefully.

He gave her a penetrating look that had her tummy squirming, then did the steps with overexaggerated moves, as though he knew she needed the help. She had to admit he reminded her of a wild eagle at the end, crouched with claws out and rapier eyes cutting the distance between them.

"Umm, okay, wow. That was... something," she murmured.

He straightened and grinned, back to being the popular kid. "Bet you can't beat that," he challenged.

Cassie's back stiffened. Did he mean because she was a girl? Determined to prove him wrong, she planted her feet and concentrated on what needed to be done. One step forward, hop, land on two feet and crouch. Ha! She looked every bit as fierce as he had. No wonder he was staring at her with growing horror...

Smack. Something hard hit her back, knocking Cassie's balance off her feet. Before she had a chance to react, Thomas was there, sliding under her body like he was rolling into home plate on the baseball field.

Instead of hitting her arms and knees on the hard gymnasium floor, she landed with a soft oomph on his chest, their faces inches apart.

For a minute, she froze, stunned he had 1. moved so fast, and 2. saved her from a hard fall. Close up she could see his eyes weren't just blue, they had a ring of green around the iris that hypnotized her. At least they did until the class started whooping and clapping like they'd just witnessed a team score a goal.

Embarrassed beyond words, Cassie scrambled to get off him just as Thomas tried to roll out from under her. Somehow, legs got crossed and she accidentally kneed him in a very bad place. He let out a great gust of air and turned pale, waiting until she awkwardly clambered free to curl into a fetal position, moaning.

Helpless, Cassie rose and stood back as Teacher hurried to kneel at Thomas's side.

"Well, that's one way to get a guy," snobby Jessica snickered from nearby.

The other kids laughed and sent Cassie snide looks while she trembled and wished they had never moved to this dumb town. Except then, she wouldn't have been saved by a real live hero.

10

Grace thanked the volunteer when she arrived, introduced her to the five preschoolers gathered around the reading castle, and waited until they were each ensconced with a book of their choice before she deemed it safe to go for a break.

She hadn't seen Kyle all morning—not that she was looking for him—okay, yes, she was. It would have been nice if he'd checked up on her, made sure she was handling the group on her own. She had, but that was beside the point. It wasn't like she was trained in childcare or anything...

Her snit had carried her down the hall in record speed and now she stood at a half-closed finger-smudged door deciding if she had the courage to walk in as though she belonged. Being an introvert had its drawbacks, but she was working on her public face as the psychologist back in Denver had called it.

Drawing a deep breath, she pushed the door open and entered, chin high. Conversation stuttered to a halt and what felt like a hundred sets of eyes zeroed in on the stranger. In reality, there were only half a dozen men and women in the room, three of each, and all wore welcoming smiles, except one, a beautiful woman around her own age, with honey-blonde hair and baby blue eyes that seemed positively glacial.

Shrugging off the shiver down her spine, Grace nodded to the group then made her way to the counter along the far wall and the coffee machine beckoning like a long-lost friend. There was a selection of pods in a revolving stand. She rotated the carousel until she found a decaf coffee, then slipped it into the machine, selected a random mug from the shelf above, hoping it didn't belong to anyone, then sighed as the rich aroma of Columbia wafted around her head. It had been a stressful morning, but she'd managed not to lose a kid or destroy the library—so far, so good. Hopefully, Cassie was having a good day, too.

Turning, she searched for an empty table and found one against the back wall, near the ice princess, but beggars couldn't be fussy. She took her steaming cup and carefully edged around the other tables and chairs, praying she didn't drip down anyone's back.

She was almost to her target when a man rose, his chair squealing on the tiles. "We have a spot here, join us." He gave her a charming smile and waved her into his seat before moving onto the next empty chair himself. "Dave Masterson, science teacher. Nice to see a pretty face around these homely mugs." He grinned at the guys around him.

"Speak for yourself, David. I only see one dog in this room," The blonde snapped, pushing her own chair back and stomping from the room.

"Ignore the Wicked Witch of Emerson. She's just bitter. So, what are you here for? Oh, wait... are you the new childcare lady?" Dave rested his arm along the back of her chair as though she'd been at the school years instead of hours.

Grace tucked her hair behind her ear and nodded. "That's me—at least for now."

"Whoa-ho, first day and the kids already have you rethinking the position. What happened? Did Billy hide the silly putty in your purse?" Another, older, man with kind eyes asked.

Grace stuttered out a surprised laugh. "Does he do that often, then?"

"Kids, you gotta love their ingenuity. Keeps the job interesting, I say." Dave chuckled. "So, are you really thinking of leaving? Kyle is right, we need this service in our community. I hope you'll reconsider."

"I didn't mean—"

"*Ms. Donovan to the office, please. Ms. Donovan to the office.*"

Grace froze, then jumped to her feet, heart plummeting to her toes. *Cassie.* "Excuse me," she murmured, hardly aware of the curious stares following her out the door. She prayed she was wrong, and it was something to do with the job, but her mother's instincts had her pace increasing until she was almost jogging down the quiet hallway, heels keeping time with her pounding pulse.

The office was empty, and she spent several frustrating moments tapping impatient fingers on the counter before a harried-looking woman with salt and pepper hair tied in a messy bun appeared from a room in the back.

"Ms. Donovan?" she enquired, drying her hands with paper towels as she came forward.

"Yes, that's me." Grace straightened and clenched her hands. "Is this about my daughter, Cassie? Is she okay?"

The woman glanced over her shoulder, then hurried to lift the countertop so Grace could pass through. "It's nothing, really. A nosebleed. It's just... it doesn't want to stop and she's a bit upset. Kyle—Mr. Roberts—thought it would help to have you join her. She's in the sickroom."

Grace's stomach tightened into a band of knots. It wasn't the first time her baby had gone through the scare of a bad nosebleed, and it wouldn't be the last, not until they beat the cancer cells attacking her body.

"Thank you," she breathed, striding past to enter the dimly lit room beyond. "How's my bab... oh, it's you." She pulled up at the sight of Kyle sitting next to a narrow bed. A thin blanket covered her daughter braced against a stack of pillows, a pile of tissues to her face, stained red.

Cassie looked at her with misery pouring out of her eyes. "Hi, Mommy," she croaked.

"Oh, punkin, what are we going to do with you?"

Kyle rose and waved her onto the chair. "I just heard she was in here myself. She's being incredibly brave. I told her I cried last time I had a nosebleed."

Grace's lips twitched at the thought of this grown man weeping over a boo-boo, but then her focus centered on her daughter. She grasped her too-small hand and leaned over to ostensibly brush the hair away from her face, but in actuality felt her forehead for fever. *Damn.*

"I didn't mean to hurt Thomas, Mr. Woberts. Am I in twouble?" Cassie stared at her principal with apprehensive eyes.

Grace glanced over her shoulder in time to see Kyle shaking his head and smiling down at her girl.

Even though she was apprehensive, something loosened in her chest. Kyle Roberts was a good man.

"I don't know the details, but I'm sure it was an accident. You don't strike me as a mischief-maker. Are you?" Kyle's wink at Grace totally destroyed his stern visage, but Cassie tightened her grip on her mom's fingers and vehemently shook her head. "No, sir."

"Well, I suggest we get you fixed up and then we'll see about apologizing to Thomas. How does that sound?"

"I'm afraid it will have to wait," Grace inserted, rising. "Cassie won't be at school for a few days."

"Aw, Mom," Cassie whined. "I don't want to go to the hospital." Proving she wasn't feeling good and knew it.

"The hospital?" Kyle asked. "For a nosebleed?"

Grace peeled the blanket away from Cas's shoulders and stepped back, waiting for her to get out of the bed, working to keep her expression calm while hopeless anger raged inside.

"This has happened before. She has a low-grade fever. Teem that up with a nosebleed that won't slow down and it's a sign her platelets have dropped. She probably needs a transfusion. I'm sorry, baby," she said when Cassie began to cry. "Come on, big girl. When it's over we'll go for a banana split—your favorite—okay?" Grace crouched and helped her daughter get her sneakers on, frowning at the gym shorts she wore. "Where are your clothes?"

"In the cha... changing room. We were in gym," Cassie hiccupped.

Kyle stepped up and held out the blanket. "Let me carry her out to the car. I'll have her clothes delivered later, and don't worry about the kids, we'll figure something out."

Grace stared at him, nonplussed. She was so used to handling Cassie's issues on her own that his offer caught her off guard.

"It's not a big deal, really," Kyle cajoled. "Let me help, Grace."

Giving in to the inevitable, she nodded and allowed him to wrap Cassie from head-to-toe in the coarse cover before gently lifting her into his arms.

"Your chariot awaits, my lady," he intoned, bowing slightly.

While Cassie giggled through her tears, all Grace could think was how tiny and fragile she looked in those masculine arms. *Please, please let her be all right.*

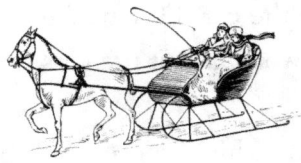

11

Sleet pelted the windshield. Just what Kyle didn't need on this day of days. If it were Friday, he would have put it down to being the thirteenth—only one too-short month to Christmas—but it was only Monday. If the rest of the week continued in the same vein it would test his resolve to quit smoking. He didn't regret his decision, as much for Avery's sake as his own, but the craving still liked to sneak up in times of stress. And between the faulty furnace, the school board's censure, and young Cassie and her mesmerizing mother, it was safe to say he was feeling the pressure.

"Do you think Cassie will be able to go home soon, Dad?"

He reached to turn up the windshield wipers and met his daughter's worried gaze in the rearview mirror. He'd debated the wisdom of taking her to the hospital, but the two girls had become fast friends. Avery would only fret if she didn't see Cassie for herself, and it would be good for Cass, as well.

"I hope so, kiddo, but our job is to cheer her up whatever the case. Can you do that?"

She glanced at the silent Thomas sitting on the passenger side before tightening the seatbelt around a cotton candy pink teddy bear wearing a tutu.

"I'm going to let Cindy stay with her, so she doesn't feel lonely."

He didn't know how he'd gotten so lucky. Even though it was just the two of them and Avery spent more time than he liked with sitters because of his job, she was a kind and caring child with a heart of gold. She definitely didn't get *that* from her mother.

"I'm sure Cindy will be a big help. You're a pretty good kid, you know." She'd received the bear—special delivery from Hollywood—on her fourth birthday. It hadn't made up for her mother not gifting it in person, but Avery treasured it anyway.

"You doing okay back there, buddy?" Kyle risked another quick glance over his shoulder, grateful traffic was light with the gloomy weather.

Thomas shrugged. He'd asked to join them tonight, but it was obvious he was second-guessing his decision now.

"Cassie will be happy to see you guys. Maybe it

will get her mind off how she's feeling." It hadn't been easy sitting them down to explain Cassie's illness after talking it over with Grace. He understood why she'd wanted to keep it private. She sought what all loving parents need—happy, healthy children who do well school. Grace wanted to protect her daughter from the inevitable questions and different attitudes sure to follow the announcement of her diagnosis.

Kyle had faith his kids would handle the situation with decorum, allowing Grace and Cassie to feel their way through what had to be a tumultuous period.

"Is Cassie really going to be okay?" Thomas asked, his voice subdued.

"Don't be silly," Avery snapped. "It's almost Christmas, isn't it? Nothing bad happens at Christmas."

If only that were true. He'd taken extra care after Samantha walked out on them to make every holiday one to remember, hence the giant sleigh in his front yard and the *Deck the Halls* decorating of their home. At first, it was hard to keep up the cheerful attitude for his daughter when all he wanted was to crawl inside a bottle of scotch and never come out. But the joy it brought to her sad little face made all the scraped knuckles and high electricity bills worthwhile. How Sam could have turned her back on her own child...

well, it gave him a new level of respect for Grace, that's all.

"Enough of that now. Don't forget, Santa's making a list, Avery Ann." Sometimes, she liked to act bossy, especially with her cousins. "How about singing me a Christmas song?"

She clapped her hands and kicked the back of his seat in excitement. "Yes, let's. Which one do you want to sing, Thomas?"

"I dunno, "Jingle Bells"?"

"Good choice, buddy. That's one of my favorites." Kyle winked into the rearview mirror, signaling onto Lamberton Street with its towering oak trees. "Let's sing it together—

> Dashing through the snow
> In a one-horse open sleigh

The kids shouted more than sang, filling the Suburban with cheer while rain pelted the roof in an off-key accompaniment.

> Jingle bells, jingle bells
> Jingle all the way.
> Oh, what fun it is to ride
> in a one-horse open sleigh,
> hey!

"Dad, do you think we could find a horse for our sleigh?"

Kyle chuckled. "Not likely, but you never know. Christmas *is* the time for miracles, right?"

"Right," the kids yelled in unison.

"I bet a sleigh ride would make Cassie feel better," Thomas said, his voice dreamy.

"A big white horse with pink ribbons in its hair," Avery inserted.

Kyle's lips twitched. "It's called a mane and what if it's a male horse?" He'd have to explain stud and mare to her when she was older—much older.

"Well, a boy horse can like pink ribbons, too. Right, Thomas? You like pink, don't ya?"

Kyle jumped in before another disagreement could begin. "My mistake. *If* we ever come across a white horse willing to pull our sleigh, we'll certainly put ribbons in his mane, okay?"

In their changing world, the kids would learn all about freedom of choice and diversity, but for today, a pink ribbon on a gelding was a good start on the road to equality.

General Hospital loomed in the distance, rain and fog turning the three-story brick building—the pride of Emerson—into a fairytale castle complete with turret. In reality, the tower held a state-of-art helicopter landing pad built for emergencies Kyle prayed his little family would never have a need to see firsthand.

"Okay, guys, remember what I told you. Inside voices, and no awkward questions to Cassie. We're here to cheer her up and that's all, got it?"

"Got it," the cousins agreed. All the cheer they'd gained from singing the Christmas carol gone as the monolith rose in front of the car.

"I wouldn't want to stay there," Thomas muttered.

Kyle couldn't agree more. He took a fortifying breath and prepared to face Grace and Cassie with an encouraging attitude while inside his stomach quaked.

***

"And then the princess held a big party, and all the village came to celebrate her safe return," Grace read aloud, her smile soft as she took in Cassie's enraptured gaze on the colorful picture book.

"Did the princess live happily ever after, Mommy?" Cassie laid back, her pale head on the thin hospital pillow breaking Grace's heart.

She set the book on the crowded bedside table and stood to tuck the blankets in, though Cass's skin was still over-warm to the touch. "Well, there were challenges ahead, but the princess had learned she was stronger than she thought, and she had her family and the whole village behind her, so yes, she did just fine."

"Will I live just fine, too?"

Grace froze in the middle of pouring water from the blue pitcher into the plastic cup that served as a lid. The last year Cassie had been through blood transfusions, chemotherapy, swollen glands, painful joints, along with a pervasive weakness and weight loss, but she'd remained positive throughout the ordeal. Her words just now scared Grace more than the disease.

Blinking back tears, she handed over the cup with a watery smile. "Of course, you will. Do you think I would let anything happen to my best girl? Now, here, drink this. You need to stay hydrated."

Cassie accepted the glass with a sigh and dutifully took a sip. "I wish we could go home. I could drink water and lie in bed, and I wouldn't get up until you said I could. Please, Mommy?"

Grace shook her head regretfully. "Sorry, munchkin. We have to wait until this bad old fever goes away, then we'll see what the oncologist has to say."

Hopefully the new anti-fungal and antibiotics, along with Neupogen—Dr. Michaels explained it as a treatment to stimulate bone marrow and build white blood cell counts—and wound cream for the burn on her thigh, would get her on the road to recovery soon. She'd spiked a 103 fever overnight though, which is why they were holding her for another day or two. Once she leveled out, Dr. Michaels planned to give her another round of platelets but worried the weight loss might stop Cassie from participating in the trial program.

Grace pinched the bridge of her nose. She had a throbbing headache thanks to the stress of the last few hours, and she hadn't dared call the school yet. She'd left those children high and dry in her rush to get Cass to the hospital. What must Kyle—Mr. Roberts—and the parents think? She could probably apply to the *Guinness Book of World Records* for shortest employment period. And now, she had to find another job, probably amongst the parents she'd disappointed.

Guilt and hopelessness beat a drum in the back of her head. If she'd only picked up on the symptoms sooner, maybe the ALL (Acute Lymphoblastic Leukemia) could have been stopped before it got a toehold in her child's chest. It was all her fault...

A soft knock on the partially closed door was preceded by Kyle's dark head peeking around the corner.

"Mind if we come in?" he said, his cheerful smile falling short of his eyes.

"Mr. Roberts," Cassie squealed, jolting up in bed. "Is Avery here?"

"She is," he answered as Grace placed a settling hand on Cassie's bony shoulder and doublechecked that she hadn't pulled any tubes out.

Avery slipped under her father's hand braced on the door and slid into the room, barely hesitating over the beeping machines before rushing to hug her friend, pink teddy bear in hand. "I was so worried," she mumbled, her face buried in the blanket. She lifted her head and grinned. "Everyone is talking about you and Thomas. Jessica is soooo jealous."

"Avery, that's enough now," her dad warned, his brows meeting over his nose even as his ears turned red. "Sorry about that, she's a gossip." He looked at Grace and shrugged awkwardly, then glanced behind him and put an arm around a handsome boy with corn-silk hair that draped across his forehead, a perfect foil for cornflower blue eyes.

Cassie stiffened beneath Grace's fingers and dropped her chin. This must be the mysterious Thomas, then. She remembered him from the puppy fair. He'd been helping his mother, Kyle's sister-in-law, with the baby while the other kids had rushed to see the animals.

Curious why the school would have linked this sweet-looking boy with her child, Grace smiled and welcomed them into the room.

"Come in, Thomas, Mr. Roberts. Cassie, look who's here." She was being overly effusive, but the sight of Kyle stepping through the doorway had thrown her off-kilter. He must have come straight from school, with his suit jacket rain- dampened and tie endearingly crooked.

"I know, Mom," Cassie mumbled, red flags of humiliation standing out on her washed-out cheeks. "Hi, Thomas," she added, shyly. "Are you... umm, okay now?"

It was Thomas's turn to light up the room like a four-alarm fire. He stared at her with are-you-kidding-me eyes before dropping his gaze to the floor and kicking at a nonexistent scuff mark. "It didn't hurt that much," he muttered, shoulders hunched.

Avery glanced from Grace to her dad and giggled. "I don't think Cassie's mom knows, Dad."

"Knows what?" Grace asked, confused.

Kyle set a beautiful bouquet of daisies on the hospital bed table and gave Cassie a reassuring look that did nothing to calm Grace's overactive imagination.

"It was nothing. A slight mishap during Phys ed, that's all. Thomas is fine, aren't you, kid?"

He gave a jerky nod and sighed. "It was an accident, Ms. Donovan, Cassie didn't mean to hurt me."

"Is this what you were talking about yesterday in the sickroom, Cass?" Grace ran her palm over her daughter's downy head.

"Yes, Mommy. Thomas saved me from a bad fall and then I accidentally kneed his... you know," she said, turning her baby blues up to Grace's bemused face.

Kyle covered a pained laugh with his hand and clasped his nephew close. "Good job, young man. When Cassie gets out of hospital, I hear she likes banana splits. Maybe we can all use a treat before Ms. Donovan has to get back to work. What do you think?"

"Cool." Thomas grinned.

"Yay!" Cassie and Avery shouted, clapping their approval.

"Shh," Grace warned, glancing at the door, smiling. "Does that mean I'm not fired?"

Kyle's brows rose comically. "Fired? Why would you think such a thing? We aren't heartless, Grace. Everyone knows you needed to be here for your girl."

She brushed tears from the corners of her eyes, the relief overwhelming. "I don't know what to say."

His warm gaze made her pulse tumble and skip through her veins. "Yes, I will go for ice cream with you, Kyle Donovan," he teased.

Blushing, she nodded. "I'd like that."

Listening to the children's chatter and Kyle's occasional comment, it was hard to regret her decision to move to Emerson. Now, if only the new treatment could give her back her daughter, the future would look promising.

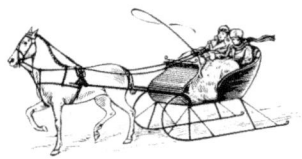

12

Kyle stared at the legal papers strewn across his desk without seeing a word. Cassie had looked so frail in that hospital bed. If it were Avery... He didn't know how Grace was keeping it together. Memories bombarded his mind. He'd been a troubled teen when his grandfather was diagnosed with Leukemia. A nagging pain in his thigh had morphed into long hospital stays, weight loss, loss of spirit, and in the end —death.

When David contacted him about setting up a grant for kids with cancer, Kyle had jumped on board. He'd received a sizable inheritance from Granddad's estate and couldn't think of a better way to invest the money. But he hadn't expected to become involved with the children who might benefit from the program. In his head, he thought he'd become a benevolent donor, who could feel good from doing a good deed. Reality was that cute little girl lying in a hospital bed fighting for her life, and her mother at her side praying for a miracle.

"Why so glum?"

Kyle looked up to see his brother standing with a shoulder propped against the doorway in a plaid shirt with sleeves rolled up to the elbows, and jeans tucked into worn work boots. The sterile white school clock on the wall behind Keith's head surprised him. He'd been daydreaming for close to an hour.

He pushed back his chair and rose. "You mean besides a faulty heater and a stubborn bathroom leak right before Christmas?" he growled. "Does that getup mean you were working on the furnace?" And hopefully fixing the darn thing, so Kyle didn't have to go to the board for more contingency funds.

Keith straightened and ambled into the room, giving the door a light kick closed. "Just call me Mr. Fix-it," he said, grinning. "You owe me a steak dinner."

"Fix the leak and I'll throw a beer into the bargain."

"Cheapskate," Keith said good-naturedly. He nodded toward the mess littering Kyle's desk. "Problems?"

"What?" Kyle frowned, then shook his head. "No, not really. Maybe. Did you receive a letter from the trustee board controlling Grandfather's estate?"

"No, why?"

"Seems there are a few clauses I wasn't aware of when I set up the hospital grant, and now they're questioning my decisions. Can they even do that?"

"I don't know, bro, but your lawyer can look into it. I'll vouch for you if that helps." Keith gave him the sympathetic smile that always scraped his nerves raw.

"I don't need my younger brother *vouching* for me, thanks." Taking his frustration out on the hapless briefcase, Kyle lifted it from the floor and slapped it down on the desk with a satisfying thunk. The temperamental snaps must have sensed he was working on his last nerve because they opened with a quiet snick.

Keith put his hand on the leather lid, holding it closed. "Why do you always do that? I'm only trying to help, not run your life. I'm not Dad, Kyle. You *can* count on me."

Keith had grease embedded in the ridges around his nails and fingers. A working man's hands. How long had it been since Kyle had used his hands for anything other than tapping away at a keyboard?

He nodded at the briefcase. "Do you mind? I have a meeting downtown in thirty minutes."

Keith heaved a sigh that rattled the blinds and took his hand away. "Whatever, man. I should have the bathroom fixed this afternoon, and then you can go on pretending life is a bed of roses. It's what you do best, after all."

Kyle ignored him to throw the papers haphazardly into the case and slam the lid shut. But guilt for his crappy attitude wouldn't let him walk out the door without some sort of an apology.

"Thanks," he murmured. "I would have been screwed without you. More times than I can count if I'm being honest. Why do you put up with me?"

"Because you're my brother. Mom said I had to love you, even if I don't always like you." Keith held out his arms and made kissy noises.

"You're an idiot, you know that?" Kyle shook his head and smiled, the anger riding him since he'd seen Cassie in the hospital easing. "Sorry I was such a dick. I appreciate the work you do around here. I'm just worried the money promised to a family in need isn't going to be delivered now. I don't know what to do."

"Is this for the Donovans, by chance?"

Kyle sank into his chair and rubbed the back of his neck. "I'm not supposed to say, but yeah. Did Thomas tell you about our visit to the hospital, then?"

Keith nodded and lowered his frame into the chair on the other side of the desk. "He wanted to know why Cassie was hooked up to so many machines." He held up his hand when Kyle opened his mouth to rebuke his brother. "Rach and I didn't tell him anything other than she probably had the flu and the machines were there to keep her safe. But that's not it, is it? Cassie Donovan has cancer, doesn't she?"

The words, said aloud like that, punched Kyle in the chest, deflating his lungs and leaving him gasping for air. Black spots floated before his eyes, and he could feel himself getting lightheaded—until a hard smack on his back shocked him into breathing again. He grasped the edge of the desk, fighting to get his equilibrium. *Cassie has cancer. Cassie has cancer. Cassie...*

"Shit, I *am* an idiot," Keith muttered from above. "I thought you knew."

Kyle waved him away, needing some space. "I do know. Why do you think this thing with the money is tearing me apart? She *needs* those treatments, dammit. Grace has so much on her plate already, the last thing she needs is to have the trustees pull the rug out from under her feet like this. There must be something I can do."

Keith shook his head. "I don't get it. The money is ours. How can they have the right to say what we do with it?"

Kyle glared at the papers hidden away in the briefcase. "Near as I can tell, Granddad wrote the will while we were still kids and had Dad notarize it. He had the clauses added to maintain control over foolish spending. Of. Which. This. Is Not." He ground his teeth, frustration building all over again.

"Well, that's it then. All you need to do is mend your bridges with dear old Dad and problem solved." Keith crossed a booted foot over a jean-clad knee and clasped hands behind his neck, as though he hadn't just suggested the impossible.

There had to be another way. He couldn't give in to his father's manipulations, it was a matter of pride.

But then, pride went before a fall, didn't it?

13

C assie slouched on the cushioned window seat and stared morosely at the wet snow floating past the dark panes of glass. She'd only seen snow once before, at her daddy's new house in Idaho. He said every flake was different, no two the same—just like people. She hadn't understood what he'd meant at the time, but she did now.

She was different.

Ever since she'd gotten out of hospital Mom hardly let her out of the house, other than a follow up doctor's appointment. She'd fallen so far behind on the Christmas concert practices she was scared she wouldn't be able to participate.

She had to participate.

Her granddad promised he would fly out so he could see her *big debut,* as he called it, and she desperately wanted him there. She was playing the recorder in choir. It was an important part and Cassie had been thrilled to get it—and terrified. She'd never done anything like this before and the thought of performing in front of a crowd made her heart race. That's why she needed to do it, though. If she could overcome her fear to act out her part in the play, then she could go to this trial Cancer program her mom wanted and beat that, too.

She just needed to convince her mom she was well enough to go back to school.

All of a sudden, a strange sight appeared on the street below. A big gray horse materialized out of the swirling snow. First his head, ears twitching and bells jingling, then a broad back and swishing tail. Then a... a Santa sleigh! Cassie blinked; sure she must be dreaming. And was that...? It was. Mr. Roberts held the reins and Avery sat at his side in a puffy pink coat and fuzzy tuque.

They stopped in front of the house!

"Mom, Mom," Cassie yelled, jumping off the bench and racing for her bedroom door. "Avery and her dad are here—in a sleigh!"

"Wha... Cassie, be careful on those stairs," her mother warned, her forbidding glare putting a damper on the excitement.

Cassie gripped the scarred railing and stared at her

mom's upturned face. "Mr. Roberts just pulled up outside with the sleigh from his front yard, and there's a horse, Mommy."

"Baby, I think you were dreaming. There are no horses in the city. See," she said, striding over to unlock and open the front door. "Nothing... What in the world?"

A burst of frosty air chilled Cassie's face as she skipped down the stairs and ran to her mother's side. "It's a real, live horse," she whispered, awed.

"Come for a ride," Avery called, bouncing up and down, smiling from ear-to-ear.

Her dad lifted a hand in greeting. He said something to Avery that had her subsiding into her seat, then wrapped the reins around a tall pole sticking up from the front of the sleigh, hopped down, and strode up the walk to the gate.

"Cassie, Grace. It's a fine night for a sleigh ride, don't you agree?" His eyes crinkled as he grinned. "You have no idea how hard it is to rent a horse on short notice."

Mommy wrapped a warm arm around her shoulders and Cassie glanced up to see an answering smile on her lips.

"I can only imagine. You're a man of many talents, Kyle Roberts."

Mr. Roberts gave a courtly bow and Avery snickered. "Daddy, you're funny."

The horse chomped at the end of the reins in his mouth, making the bells jingle. Mr. Roberts glanced over his shoulder before raising his brows at Mommy.

"So, are you up for a plodding tour of the neighborhood?"

The arm around Cassie's shoulders tightened and her stomach plunged.

"I don't think it's a good idea, Kyle. Cass—"

Cassie grabbed her mom's hand and tugged to get her attention. "Mommy, please. Just for a little while..."

Mom's fingers were like icicles tracing Cass's cheek. "Honey, you just got out of hospital—"

"A week ago, Mom. I've been stuck inside the house ever since." Tears hovered on her lashes. "I want to go, please!"

Mr. Roberts opened the creaky gate and took a step closer. "Grace, I brought a warm blanket and a thermos of hot chocolate. We won't go far, just around the block."

Mom hesitated, then sighed. "I suppose it won't hurt, as long as you stay covered up, young lady." She tipped Cas's chin up and dropped a kiss on her nose.

Bubbles erupted in Cassie's chest, and she fist bumped the sky. "Yay! I get to go, Avery." She turned to race into the house. "Wait for me, I need my coat and boots."

Mr. Robert's chuckle and her friend's shout of glee followed her into the house—she was going to ride on Santa's sleigh!

CASSIE'S EXCITEMENT made the effort of locating a horse to rent—from a friend of a friend of Keith's—and hurrying to get the old sleigh in shape to be pulled, worthwhile. When Thomas and Avery came up with the idea, Kyle had shrugged it off. Cassie hadn't returned to school since leaving the hospital, and Grace was close-lipped about her condition, other than to say she was on the mend. At least Grace had come back to work, leaving Cass with the kindly owner of the house she rented. It relieved some of his short-staffing issues, but he needed to come up with a way to bring more staff to the school. They were already running with overflowing classrooms and a serious lack of substitutes should any of his teachers become ill— and since they were in the middle of flu season...

But he'd worry about that tomorrow. Tonight, was all about showing Emerson's hidden beauty to the Donovan ladies. Except, Grace stood on the doorstep, arms wrapped around her body, trying not to shiver as she anxiously stared at the big gray placidly chewing his bit as snow covered the broad back.

"He's as calm as they come, don't worry."

Her gaze shot to his and back to their delipidated chariot. "Actually, I was wondering if you need a license to operate heavy machinery for that get-up." Her quick smile sent heat flickering through his veins. Tired and stressed as she was, Grace Donovan was still a beautiful woman.

"I figured I'd bribe the authorities with concert tickets and remind them it's the season of generosity— think it'll work?"

She laughed outright, her pretty eyes sparkling. "It's worth a try. After all, it is Santa's sleigh you're hauling." She glanced over her shoulder as Cassie breezed through the doorway, coat half-on, and hat squashed over her ears. "Okay, well, have a good time, and stay under those covers, missy." Snagging the loose arm on Cassie's jacket, she helped her daughter get ready, then gave her a hug. "Love you to the moon and back."

"Love you to the bottom of the ocean and up to the sky, Momma," Cassie answered before running past Kyle toward the sleigh.

"Slow down," he and Grace called at the same time.

"You'll scare the horse," Grace warned, stepping

off the porch, her hand outstretched as though she could grab her daughter's shoulder and pull her back from the perceived danger.

Cassie slowed to a crawl and crept to the side of the sleigh like it might disappear. Avery leaped forward, pointed out the foothold, and giggled as Cassie half fell into the sled.

Once he knew they were safely settled on the backseat, he turned to Grace. "Better hurry, they aren't going to sit still for long." He grinned.

Her eyes widened comically. "Me? On a horse? Thanks, but no thanks."

"It's okay, I'll let you ride in the sleigh," he teased. All the challenges she'd been through, and she balked at an old gray nag? Go figure.

"You need to work on that humor of yours, Mr. Roberts." She frowned at the curlicue rails and red velvet seats. "Where would I sit?"

Kyle's smile grew. "With me, of course."

Grace rolled her eyes. "Is that your best pick-up line?"

"Are you looking for a line?" Suddenly the conversation had taken a turn for the interesting.

"Of course not," she stated just a little too adamantly, and tossed her head. "I don't have time for dating." The moment the words left her lips, she covered her mouth and looked at him with wide eyes.

"Not that you were asking. I'm sorry, I don't know why I said such a thing."

Kyle grinned, enjoying the flare of embarrassment adding some much-needed color along sculpted cheekbones. "Oh, I'm asking," he said, determined she should be aware of his interest. "I think you're a remarkable woman, Grace Donovan. One I want to know better."

He moved a step closer, bumping into her personal space, feeling the electricity spark between them, and by the dilation of her pupils, she felt it too.

Brushing golden strands of hair behind her ear, he took a deep breath and slowly let it go. "I won't lie, if our kids weren't watching I would definitely be kissing you right now."

Her mouth rounded into a startled *oh* that set his pulse pounding. "What are you trying to do to me, Kyle?"

His lips quirked as he stepped back, giving her some room. "If you don't know, I'm doing it wrong. Get your coat, Grace. Your chariot awaits."

14

The gentle swaying of the sleigh brought Grace into constant contact with Kyle on the surprisingly comfortable front bench. Her gaze kept sliding to the leather reins held loosely between his strong, masculine hands. For a man with a career behind a desk, he was surprisingly fit with a lean waist and broad shoulders that made her feel sheltered. After years of struggling alone, it was tempting to lean on his strength and let him bear the weight, if only for a little while.

He turned his head and caught her staring. "Having a good time?"

Snowflakes kissed his dark hair before melting away, only to be replaced with more as though the heavens themselves blessed this god among men.

She blinked away the fanciful thoughts and

glanced at the two girls in the backseat giggling under the blanket. "They are. I can't thank you enough for this, Kyle."

Instead of the expected smile, his brows lowered and those full, sensuous lips she couldn't stop looking at firmed into a straight line.

"I don't need your gratitude, Grace. Thomas and Avery wanted to do something special for their friend, that's all there is to it. Make no mistake, I'm not a saint."

Unaccountably hurt, she straightened and edged away from him. "I didn't mean to upset you. It's just that, with my husband's death and Cassie's... well, there haven't been many happy moments lately for her. This ride, it means a lot."

He covered her knee with his hand, stoking the awareness smoldering in her veins.

"Forgive me?" He squeezed, then returned to guiding the horse around a trio of snow-covered parked cars on the street. "I don't usually speak to beautiful women so rudely. I guess the *joie de vivre* the holidays are supposed to instill hasn't caught up to me yet."

He found her beautiful? It had been years since she'd thought of herself as anything other than a mother. She didn't know what to do with his revelation. Pretend she hadn't heard him? Gush like a schoolgirl? Climb into the backseat with the girls before she did something crazy like kissing his stubbly cheek?

"Am I scaring you away?" he asked, shooting her a rueful glance.

"What?" she asked, startled out of fantasizing about her boss. "Umm, no, of course not. I was just thinking it's been a long time since I've been ice skating. Do you have an indoor rink in the area?"

"Skating," Avery piped up from the back. "Daddy, can we go? Please?"

Kyle arched his brow, lips quirking. "Look what you've started now."

Grace shrugged, feeling surprisingly lighthearted. "Is that a yes?"

"Yeah, say yes," the girls urged, making the sleigh rock with their enthusiasm.

"There's a manmade rink downtown on the front lawn of the Cyprus Hotel. They sell hot chocolate and mittens with the entry tickets and donate the money to food hampers—it's a good cause." He pulled back on the reins, calling, "Whoa, boy," and turned on the seat until their knees brushed together. "Are you sure you can skate? I don't want to be seen with an amateur, it's bad for my image, you know."

She chortled. "Is that right? I guess you'll just have to wait and see, won't you?"

"Mommy is a great skater. She's won ribbons," Cassie pressed, eavesdropping.

"Cass, what did I tell you about listening in on adult conversations?"

Cassie looked sheepish for all of two seconds. "To mind my own business, but this is different—it's skating!"

Kyle covered his mouth to stifle a chuckle. "She's got you there, Mom."

Grace couldn't believe she'd suggested skating. Between the snow cocooning them on a winter sleigh and holiday lights glittering on homes up and down the block, it felt like a moment out of time—a place where reality faded, and nostalgia took its place.

If only they could stay in this happy little bubble forever.

"Are you up to an hour's exertion?" She scanned Cass's face. Her daughter had rosy cheeks and sparkling eyes, but she had a feeling it was more to do with the Roberts family than fever.

Cassie nodded vigorously, the pom-pom on her toque bouncing this way and that. "I promise not to overdo it. Avery says there are picnic tables set up all around the rink, so people can rest. Come on, Mom. We never do anything."

If she had a dollar for every time she'd heard that in her life...

But it was true, since Cassie became ill the only excitement in their lives were the multiple trips back and forth to hospitals and cancer clinics.

"Okay, let's do it," she said, and was gratified to see a wide smile spread over Cassie and Avery's countenances amid cheers of glee. She looked at Kyle, and her heart fluttered. "I guess that's a yes."

He stared at her for a moment, approval—and something harder to pinpoint—softening his jaw and adding a warm glint to eyes as dark as the nighttime sky.

"You are full of surprises, Grace. I think I have you figured out, and then you slip me a curveball and I'm left standing at the plate wondering what just happened. It's... exhilarating."

Without giving her time to process his pronouncement, he clucked his tongue, gave the reins a light snap over the horse's rump, and continued down the street, whistling off-key while the girls sang in the backseat.

Grace tucked trembling fingers between her knees and pretended it wasn't her who'd just been given a homerun.

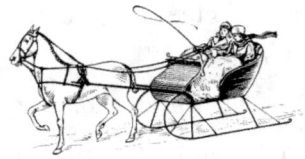

15

Kyle tightened the laces on Avery's skates, while keeping an eye out for the rest of their party at the busy ice rink. Grace had called to say she'd meet him at the entrance and Keith was bringing his family after Thomas missed out on the sleigh ride the night before due to basketball practice. Kyle didn't want to delve into why his hands were sweaty even though the night air was chilly coming off the rink. Or why his heartbeat ricocheted like a pinball when she suddenly appeared, blond hair pulled back in a ponytail that made her look too young to have a six-year-old daughter, and pink gloss on bow-shaped lips. Cassie held her hand in a puffy cotton candy coat and a snowflake toque over her shorn head.

"They're here," he said, just as Keith arrived with Rachel and Thomas.

Avery jumped up and waved her hands above her head. "Over here," she called, wobbling on the blades of her figure skates. "Daddy, they can't see us."

Kyle grasped her arm. "Sure, they do. Look, Uncle Keith is showing them where we are." It was true, his brother had an arm wrapped around Grace and his wife, guiding them through the thick crowd congested at the entrance with Cassie and an uncomfortable looking Thomas trailing behind.

The pleasure that flashed in Grace's quicksilver eyes as they approached went a long way to easing the needless spike of jealousy he felt at Keith's lingering touch. Ridiculous. He knew his brother loved his wife with all his heart, but...

"Quit giving us the stink-eye, bro, we're only a few minutes late. This place is a zoo."

"Where's little man?" Kyle smiled at Rachel and tugged Thomas's cap over his eyes.

"He's staying with his grandparents tonight. Keith decided we shouldn't have all the fun of caring for a baby." A husky laugh burbled from her throat. "I figure we'll get a call to go pick him up before midnight."

"'O, ye of little faith." Keith released Grace and kissed his wife. "They raised their own two little hellions, didn't they?"

"Yes," she agreed. "That's what has me worried."

"Hey," Kyle protested. "Don't lump me with this vagabond. I'm the good twin, remember?"

Keith gave him a light shove. "In your dreams, bucko." He glanced around the rink with its disco ball and twinkling lights. Holiday music played from monster-sized black speakers stacked like building blocks at opposing ends of the football sized arena. A giant tent gave the setting a sense of intimacy while protecting visitors from the elements. Nearby the ocean swelled and slapped against the docks, spraying the air with a pungent tang of salt and decay.

"They went all out this year. The disco ball is a nice touch."

"A bit too 80's for my taste, but the crowd seems to be enjoying it." A couple glided by, their skates barely touching the ice as they twirled and swayed to the music.

Kyle turned to Grace and Cassie. "Ready to tear up the proverbial dance floor?"

"This is so much better than an indoor arena. The atmosphere alone is worth the price of admission." Grace's expression mirrored the wonder on her daughter's face.

His neck grew hot. "Oh, damn. I meant to buy. Some date I turned out to be."

"Don't worry, bro. I covered it. You can get the hot

chocolate later." Keith flashed him a wicked grin, then went back to tying Thomas's hockey skates.

Brothers. Kyle grimaced, then looked at Grace. "I'm sorry. You must think I'm a jerk."

"I don't think that at all. It wasn't a real date, anyway. We work together. You're my boss. I'd like to think we're friends." She glanced over to the picnic table where Keith had started in on Cass's skates, carefully tightening the pink laces before giving them a pretty bow. Avery and Thomas edged toward one of three openings in the low railing that bordered the rink until Rachel called for them to wait. They reluctantly came back and hovered over Keith's shoulder, thereby making a two-minute job twice as long. Finally, the kids were ready, and with a quick wave to their parents they wobbled to the ice, then took off, arms out at their sides for balance. Instead of fear, their expressions were of pure joy and youthful exuberance. A few of their classmates were out on the rink and soon a group formed, some holding the rails, while others took to the ice like ducks to water.

"I like you, Kyle. A lot. You've brought a smile to my girl's face. I can't tell you what that means to me. I'm glad we made the decision to move to Emerson, even if it was thanks to an anonymous benefactor." Grace blinked tear-bright eyes and gestured to the rink. "You mentioned a dance?"

Kyle wiped the dismay from his expression and smiled. "After you, Twinkle toes." Talk about hoisted with his own petard. Thanks to the donation he'd given to the cancer clinic, a donation that could be reneged at any moment, Grace and her sweet child had entered his life. But when they found out he'd hidden it from them, they would be hurt, and the trust he'd built between them would be broken.

Damn his father anyway.

CASS STEP-GLIDED around the outside edge of the skating rink, sticking close enough to the rails to save herself if she tripped, and far enough away the more experienced kids in their group couldn't mock her. She kind of wished they would leave so Avery and Thomas would pay more attention to her. They were way ahead of her now, laughing and chattering without a care in the world. She knew Avery wasn't doing it on purpose, it was that dumb old Jessica. She looked like a doll in her skating costume and had been quick to brag she was in figure skating classes—of course, she was— and the star of the Christmas pageant. It wasn't that Cass was jealous—though the hard ball in her stomach said otherwise—it was just girls like Jessica made her mad. They had everything. Friends. Family.

Health.

Much as Cass tried to act like everything was all right for her mom's sake, inside she was scared. Some of the kids in hospital were sick, like really sick, and their parents seemed so sad. She didn't want that for her mom. And if she didn't make it, then what? Did she just go to sleep and never wake up? Did angels come and take her away, like Daddy? She'd seen the angel that day. Her dad was sleeping on the couch when she came. First there was a brilliant white light. It filled the room and hurt Cass's eyes. But then a lady appeared from right out of the ceiling. She had fluffy wings and a kind smile. Instead of being frightened, Cass smiled back. She tried to stay awake and see what the pretty lady wanted, but her eyes grew heavy. When she woke up, her mom was there with tears streaking her cheeks and Cass had known—her dad was gone.

It took a long time for Mommy to laugh like she did with Mr. Roberts. Cass didn't want to be the reason her mom quit. Which meant she had to get better. *She had to.*

"Hey, new girl," Jessica called, sidling up beside her like they were fast friends. "Haven't you skated before?"

Cass refused to let Jessica rile her, and kept her gaze focused straight ahead. "Yes, but not for a long time. I'm just being careful." *So go away.*

"You need to take longer strides. Sweep your feet, like this, see?" Jessica took off, her swirly skirt shimmering under the big round dome hanging from the center of the rink. Cass had to give her credit; she did *seem* like she knew what she was doing. Her feet kind of hop-skipped over the ice, then she gave a quick twist to her legs and came to a skidding stop, a smug grin on her lips.

"Your turn," she yelled, catching the attention of Avery, Thomas, and all the other kids in their group.

Great, now she didn't have a choice. If she didn't want to look like a dork, Cass was going to have to perform a maneuver at least as good as Jessica's. She hadn't lied, she used to skate back before... but her legs were weaker now—so was her confidence.

There was only one thing to do.

Closing her eyes, Cassie sent up a silent prayer she could pull this off. Then she opened her eyes, and with single-minded determination, gritted her teeth and pushed off with her back foot. One step, two steps, her stride lengthened and before long she was gliding. Right past a glowering Jessica. Around Avery and a stunned-looking Thomas. Faster and faster, she went until the rail was little more than a blur. Maybe she wasn't a fancy figure skater like Jessica, but Cass wasn't a quitter. Giving up meant defeat and in her case, that was nonnegotiable. There was too much riding on the outcome.

As she came up on one of the entry points for the rink, Mommy and Mr. Roberts stepped onto the ice, laughing until they saw her barreling toward them.

"Cassie, what in the world?" Mom cried just before Cass crashed into her legs, knocking them both off-balance. Mom's arms windmilled, trying to stop their fall, and Mr. Roberts reached out, his fingers grasping the back of Cass's coat as her mom went down, her head smacking the ice with a dull thud.

"Mommy," Cass sobbed, falling to her knees, and crawling to her mother's side. "I'm sorry, I'm sorry, I'm s...s... sorry."

Mom groaned and tried to rise, lifting a trembling hand to the back of her skull, but Mr. Roberts gently pushed her down and used his coat to pillow her head.

"Take it easy, now. Rest for a minute. You've had quite the collision." He gave Cassie a reassuring look. "She's going to be fine, honey. What about you? Did you get hurt?"

"Cassie, baby, are you okay? What were you thinking?" Mom held out her hand and Cassie grabbed on, tears running down her face. A crowd had gathered around them, including Avery, Thomas, and Jessica, but Cass wasn't feeling triumphant anymore. She'd been the dumb one for giving in to Jessica's razzing.

And now her mom was hurt because of her. Guilt and fear churned in her tummy.

"I... I think I'm going to be sick," she whispered, and promptly bent over and lost her dinner on the ice.

In front of all those people.

Her life sucked.

16

G race frowned at the masculine hand gently nudging her awake. She was so tired. The last few weeks' worth of stress had caught up to her. "Go away," she mumbled.

A husky laugh greeted her grumbles. "Come on, princess. Doctor's orders. I'm supposed to check on you regularly throughout the night, remember?"

She groaned and lifted weighted eyelids. Dark bedroom furniture and a plaid robe hanging from a hook over the door told her she wasn't in her own home if the pine-scented sheets and man's watch on the bedside table didn't give it away.

She turned on the plump pillow and winced. "My head is killing me." A careful probing with her fingertips pinpointed the injury, a tender lump on the crown of her head. "Where am I?"

Kyle frowned and touched her brow. "Amnesia wasn't listed as one of the issues to watch for in patients suffering from a slight concussion." He held up his hand. "How many fingers do you see?"

"All of them," she answered promptly, working to lever herself into a sitting position. Kyle rose from the recliner he'd pulled up to the bed and leaned over to grab the spare pillow on the other side of the bed. She sucked in a sharp breath; senses bombarded by virile male. His weight settled on her chest, cocooning her into the mattress, even as her breasts swelled, and nipples hardened in an embarrassing rush she was sure he couldn't miss.

He stilled, staring into her eyes, his own darkening in response to her reaction. "Grace—" His mouth hovered a hairsbreadth away, drawing her lips like a lodestone.

"Where is Cassie?" Grace blurted, throwing up mental blocks to combat her body's weakness.

Kyle dragged down on her bottom lip with his thumb, igniting a rush of dark urgings within. "You can't ignore what's happening between us forever," he murmured, hypnotizing her with the husky timber of his voice. His hand slid behind to cradle her neck, making her heart beat like a caged bird, and lifted her head to ... slide the pillow into place.

He straightened and resumed his seat in the

recliner, the lamp on the bedside table throwing his face into shadow. "Cassie is upstairs fast asleep in the spare bedroom. She wanted to stay here with you, but I persuaded her to get some rest. Poor kid blames herself for your injury. You've raised an amazing child, Grace."

Her emotions see-sawing between dragging him into her/his bed and throwing back the covers to run from the room, she took a moment to assimilate his words, but worry overrode everything else. "It's not her fault. I need to go to her, make sure she's all right."

Once again, she tried to sit up, this time getting as far as to throw her legs—bare, she was startled to find— over the side of the bed before Kyle leaned forward and stopped her with a well-placed hand on her thigh.

"Tomorrow, Grace. She's fine, I promise." He squeezed her leg, urging her to lie down. "You'd only worry her more right now. After a good night's rest, you'll be in a better position to reassure your daughter of your SuperMom powers."

Reluctantly, she gave in and flopped back, immediately regretting it as her head hit the pillow. "Ooh," she moaned, clasping the sides of her skull.

"Damn stubborn woman," Kyle muttered. He uncapped a prescription bottle and dumped two pills into his hand. "Here, take these. The doctor said it would help with the pain." He dropped them onto her open palm, then slipped an arm behind her back to brace her while she swallowed the pills and chased them with a drink of water.

"Better?" he asked, taking the glass to set it on the table before settling her against the pillows without banging her poor head.

"Yes, thank you," she said grudgingly. She sounded ungrateful when she was just the opposite. He'd put himself out for her and Cassie—even going so far as to give up his bed. At least...

"Where are *you* going to sleep?"

KYLE ADDED vanilla and cinnamon to the bowl of scrambled eggs and milk, gave it all a brisk whisk, then dunked a thick slice of bread into the mixture. He pulled the dripping concoction out of the bowl and added it to the ones already sizzling on the hot grill.

"Breakfast time, ladies," he called, flipping two golden brown French Toast slices onto plates and sprinkling icing sugar over the top.

"Smells delicious," Grace said, startling him into almost dropping the spatula.

He turned and smiled, even as his pulse spiked. She'd wrapped his robe over the T-shirt he'd dressed her in to sleep. The acetaminophen administered at the hospital had made her too groggy to manage on her own, so he'd stepped in to help—he was such a gentleman he'd even kept his eyes closed, mostly.

"Good morning. How's the head?"

She shrugged, suppressing a barely noticeable wince. "It's been better." She eyed the coffee machine and box of dark roast pods. "May I?"

"Of course," he said, standing with a plate in one hand, spatula in the other like an idiot. "Cups are in the cupboard to the right." And now he had a too-close-to-naked-for-comfort woman brushing past him in his suddenly too-small kitchen. How could she smell so good after the night she'd been through? Like roses and... lavender? No, vanilla. Toasty brown and...

"I think you're burning something," she said, her lips twitching as coffee gurgled and brewed in the background.

"Hmmm?" he murmured, his gaze on the fine wisps of hair kissing her nape. Then her words sank in, and he whipped around, mortified to see smoke rising from the grill. "Oh, sh... shoot," he growled as Avery and Cassie rushed into the room and the smoke detector gave off an ear-splitting shriek.

"Fire, fire," Avery yelled at the top of her lungs, notifying the neighborhood of his blunder.

"There's no fire," he huffed, batting at the smoke with a dishtowel. "Avery, bring the stepstool. Run."

Grace hurried to the stove, shut off the offending burner, and used an oven mitt to move the grill off to the side where the heat was less intense. Cassie stood near the doorway, her eyes huge and a big smile on her petite face.

Kyle might have found the situation amusing, as well, if he hadn't been the one to burn their breakfast. He waved the towel in the air like a white flag, hoping to disperse enough smoke to make the noise box above his head shut down. This was one of those times he wished he'd been born with a few extra inches.

Finally, Avery dragged the white stool into the room. He hurried up the two steps to disconnect the battery and breathed a sigh of relief when the shrill ringing stopped. "Well, that was an adventure," he muttered.

"Daddy, I forgot to tell you Jessica's mom was at the door. I let her in before I grabbed the stool. Can we go play now?"

Kyle jerked around and almost fell off the stool. Tammy Bigalow stood next to a diminutive Grace— sexy and disheveled in his robe—a look of dismay on her perfectly made-up face. Tammy, whose father ran the school board with an iron fist. Tammy, who made no secret of her plans to become the next Mrs. Roberts.

Just shoot me now.

Sending up a quick prayer for fortitude, Kyle

hopped down and smiled at his scowling guest. "Tammy, what a surprise. As you can see, we've had an entertaining start to the day. I should stick to teaching and leave the cooking to those who know how." He chuckled half-heartedly before answering his daughter. "You can play *quietly* in your room for half an hour, but then it's breakfast time. We have school today."

Cassie cast a doubtful glance on the overdone toast. "Do you have cereal?"

"Cass," her mother warned, curling her bare toes under the drooping ends of the robe. "We'll talk about manners later. Make sure you bring all your stuff downstairs before we have to leave."

"Okay," Cass said, trailing behind Avery with slumped shoulders.

Kyle broke the awkward silence by offering Tammy a drink. "I have coffee, tea, milk…"

"Nothing, thank you." Tammy raised her chin and stepped away from Grace to trail long red nails over the kitchen island with the debris from his cooking attempt spread over the top like an admission of guilt.

"I had no idea you were so… homey," she murmured, her gaze dark and vindictive.

Kyle glanced at Grace to see how she was coping with this invasion—not well—then smiled disarmingly. "I have a feeling this isn't a social call. Was there something you needed?"

Tammy turned and posed against the counter, reaching out to stroke his button-down shirt front. "I didn't realize I needed to call before making an appearance, darling. I rather thought we were beyond those niceties."

Kyle stopped her wandering fingers, his hand closing over hers to give a gentle squeeze. "I haven't had my first coffee yet, it's too early for games. What is this about, Tammy?"

She took a step back, pouting. "I thought it was worth a try." She shot Grace a hot look. "He's not into long-term, you know."

Grace set her cup in the sink, then turned to leave. "I'll let you two have some privacy. I need to get ready for work. Nice to see you again, Ms. Bigalow."

"Grace—" Kyle hesitated, guessing what she was thinking and not sure how to explain without making things worse.

"Let her go, dear. We have so much to talk about." Tammy put a proprietary hand on his shoulder, sealing their non-relationship in Grace's eyes.

"I've got to go," Grace said, her face set. She strode through the doorway with her head high and disappeared from sight.

Kyle swore under his breath and dropped his shoulder, breaking free of the piranha's grip. "I know why you're here. Jessica told you about the skating rink, didn't she?"

Tammy lost the beguiling expression, her gaze turning brittle. "She's my daughter, of course she would tell me when she sees her principal. Imagine my surprise when she relayed you were on a date with the babysitter—how... quaint."

Kyle crossed his arms and leaned back on his heels. "Not that it's any of your business, but Grace and I are friends. When she fell, she suffered a slight concussion. I offered to watch her overnight and care for Cassie— end of story." If he didn't put an end to her conjectures, it could mean real trouble for both of them. He could handle it. He wasn't so sure about Grace.

"I hope you know what you're doing, Kyle. Daddy told me about the inheritance you spent on getting Grace's child into that program. It's commendable of you, but also foolhardy. The school board doesn't approve of your recent decisions. You better be careful or..."

Cold, hard anger suffused Kyle's chest. He'd done nothing wrong. A young family had needed help and he'd stepped up to the plate. If that was a mistake, then so be it. He would do the same thing again. But how could his father have gone behind his back to the school board the way he had? That was reprehensible.

"Tammy, I really need to get ready for work. You can see yourself out, I'm sure."

"Well, I've never," she spouted, turning on a dime and marching for the front door. "You haven't heard the last of this," she warned before slamming the door.

No, but he sure as hell was going to put an end to it once and for all.

Digging his cell out, he began dialing his father as he walked into the hall... and froze. Grace stood there, her face white and tears dripping down her cheeks.

"It was you," she said.

17

Cassie scooted backward on hands and feet until her back hit the wall. She stared at Avery, her stomach in knots. She didn't understand everything that had been said downstairs, but she knew it wasn't good. They'd been having so much fun until Jessica's mom showed up and wrecked it. And now her mom was standing in the hallway crying and Cass didn't know what to do.

Avery wrapped an arm around her neck and pulled her in for a hug. "Don't worry, my dad will fix this."

"Sure, but it's your dad that made Mommy cry. You heard her." Cass broke free and rose, wiping at her wet eyes and running nose. "I don't want to move again. We won't be friends anymore!"

Avery slowly stood and faced her. "Why would

you need to move? And besides, it's my dad who's in trouble, not your mom."

Cass reared back, "That's not our fault."

"I never said it was." Avery shook her head and sighed. "Look, I'm not trying to fight. We need to stick together. You don't want to leave Emerson, right?"

"Right," Cass agreed, scratching nervously at her arms.

"And I don't want my dad to lose his job. We need to find a way to help them. Are you with me?" Avery lifted her hand, her smile encouraging Cass to believe.

She smacked her friend's hand, though she was filled with doubt. They were two kids. How were they going to make a difference?

Avery tiptoed to the railing and peeked over the top, then whirled around. "They're gone. Let's go." She ran to the head of the stairs and glanced over her shoulder, excitement glimmering in her eyes. "Hurry. They might come back."

Left with little choice, Cass followed her down the stairs, freezing when the third tread down creaked. Her heart jumped into her throat, and they hadn't even done anything yet.

"This is a bad idea," she stage-whispered, her hand cupped to her mouth.

"Shhh," Avery hissed. "Do you want to get us in trouble?"

Cass was pretty sure they were already crossing that bridge... and the river was flooding. And they weren't wearing life jackets. But she was committed. If there was even the slightest chance Avery knew a way to bring their parents back together, she had to try.

So, she swiftly and silently ghosted down the rest of the stairs and into the entry where the boots lay on their sides and coats hung from pegs on the wall. Looking down, she realized she was still wearing the pj's she'd borrowed from Avery.

"I'm not dressed," she breathed, trying her hardest to keep quiet this time.

"Neither am I. We aren't going far, don't worry." Avery already had her pink gumboots pulled on and was reaching for her puffy jacket. The material made a weird noise, like fingers on a balloon, and once again they froze.

Cass could hear Mr. Roberts murmuring down the hall in his bedroom, but nothing from her mom. Scared now, she hurried into her own outdoor clothing, the boots pushing the legs of her pajama bottoms up, so they resembled colorful mushrooms. If her classmates saw her, she'd really be a laughingstock, but she couldn't worry about that now.

They were on a mission.

"Okay, let's go." Avery carefully opened the door

while Cass crossed her fingers it didn't squeak, and then slipped through the narrow opening.

She took one last glance down the hall, then followed her friend. They had to make things right. *They just had to.*

KYLE DRUMMED his fingers on the small desk in his bedroom, the ring of the cellphone in his ear ramping up his tension along with the firmly closed door of the ensuite bathroom. He'd begged Grace to listen to his rationalization for what he had done, but she was hurting, and he couldn't blame her. Damn Tammy Bigalow and her interference. It had broken his heart to see Grace crying and know he was the cause. The only thing he could do to make things right was something he should have done to begin with.

"Senator Roberts office, how may I help you?"

He straightened at the sound of his father's trusted receptionist on the line. "Claire, it's Kyle Roberts. Is he in?"

The impersonal tone dropped, and her slight brogue became more pronounced. "Well then, it's been a wee while, Mr. Kyle. And how is the little one?"

"Not so little," he replied, smiling. Claire was a

treasure. His father didn't deserve her. "She's almost seven and more of a handful than I ever was."

Claire chuckled. "I doubt that's possible. When are you going to come into the office, child? It's been too long."

Never, if he could help it. "Seattle is too far away for me to drop in, but maybe one day I can make an exception—for you."

"Oh, you charmer, you. Isn't it time you gave that sweet little girl a sister? Life is too short for regrets, my boy."

He'd been thinking the same since meeting Grace, but now... He glanced at the bathroom door, the sound of his shower setting his imagination on fire. Soft, pearly skin and the long, curvaceous lines of Grace's back. Hips. Legs...

"Kyle, are you still there?"

Claire's voice pierced the sensual fog in his mind. Heat stained his cheeks, even though it was impossible for the elderly woman to know what he'd been thinking.

"Sorry," he said, wincing at his raspy throat. "Lots on my mind."

There was a pregnant pause. He dropped his head, suddenly taken back to his awkward teenage days.

"Yes, well, your father can take your call now. I'll put you through."

"Thank you, Claire. I appreciate it."

"Take care of yourself and that darling child, Mr. Kyle."

Click, enough silence to make his hands clench, then, "So, you've deigned to call after all this time, have you? Why, I wonder?"

"Maybe because I miss you, Father. Isn't that a good enough reason?" Why did they have to continually strike sparks off one another? Grandpa had been the buffer between them when he was alive, but now... now there was animosity.

"I hope you don't want me to swallow your gibberish, it's too early in the morning for bitters."

"Always with the condescending attitude, *Dad*. And yes, your granddaughter is fine, thank you very much for asking."

Another phone rang in the background and Kyle fully expected their call to end. Instead, his father cleared his throat and lowered his voice. "How is she, really?"

"Avery, Dad. Mom would have loved knowing they shared the same name, and so should you."

"I do, dammit. Don't put words in my mouth."

Kyle shook his head. Why did he bother? "*She* is good. Great, even. Which you would know if you ever came to visit. The fancy gifts you send don't make up for your lack of presence in her life, but that's not the reason for my call. I need you to back off and let me spend my inheritance the way I see fit. Grandpa would have wanted me to help others with cancer, you know he would. This program is important to me, Dad, let me have it."

He held his breath—waiting—and suddenly noticed the shower had stopped and the door was open. Grace stood in the entry, his robe hugging her the way he wanted to, with damp tendrils of hair caressing her neck and trailing onto the enticing vee of her chest. But it was her expression that held him spellbound. Liquid heat spilled from her eyes and warmed his chest. She'd heard at least part of his justification to his dad, and she forgave him. Relief coursed through his veins. He held out his hand and she walked right into his arms, her head fitting snuggly under his chin. A heavy weight lifted, and he felt lighter—happy, as he hadn't in a very long time.

"I only want what's best for you, son," his dad was saying. "But if it's what you truly want—"

"It is," Kyle stated, curving his hand around her waist and pressing a soft kiss to her forehead. "It's exactly what I want."

"All right, then. I'll clear the funds immediately. And Kyle... expect me for Christmas."

Kyle fumbled the phone, not sure he'd heard right. Joy and trepidation tap-danced over his heart with elation coming out on top. "Great. That's great. We look forward to seeing you in a couple of weeks, then. Bye."

"Give Avery a hug from her grandfather."

"I will, Dad."

He set the phone aside and tipped his head back, tears leaking from the corners of his eyes. All these years, and finally, maybe, they could become a real family. It was a lot to absorb.

"Are you okay?" Grace murmured, her hand on his throat where it convulsed with pent up emotion.

He looked down into her beautiful eyes and smiled. "I'm better than okay. Now."

He bent and kissed her velvet-soft lips, groaning when she opened for him to delve inside. "I'm sorry I wasn't straight with you right from the start. I didn't know who the recipient would be until Cassie enrolled at my school. I should have come to you then, but I didn't want to do anything to scare you away."

He brushed a damp lock of hair behind her ear and kissed her again. "She deserves this chance, Grace. I want to help, will you let me in?"

She reached up and pulled his head down. "Shut up and kiss me."

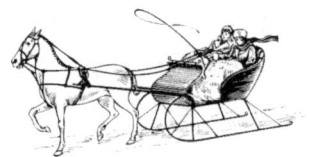

18

Grace watched Kyle over the rim of her cup as he worked to make Cassie and Avery healthy school lunches. She'd offered to help, but he'd gently insisted he could handle a sandwich or two, so she'd cleaned the mess from earlier, and made them each a coffee.

Funny how life could lead you down paths you never expected.

If not for Kyle's generosity, they would never have heard of Emerson. Cassie would have missed out on her chance to get better and the friendships she'd gained along the way, and Grace wouldn't have met a man she could easily fall in love with.

Second chances.

After David passed away, it had taken a long time to get her feet under her again. He was everywhere. In her thoughts, her dreams, their daughter's eyes. Some days, the agony had been almost more than she could bear. Then slowly, minute-by-minute, hour-by-hour the memories softened, becoming something to be cherished. Treasured and taken out at special times to reminisce and laugh and maybe even shed a few tears over. He would always have a place in her heart, but she'd come to realize there was room for fresh starts and new celebrations.

From the moment they'd arrived in Emerson—and even before—Kyle had been in their corner. He was a good man with a kind heart, she should never have doubted him.

"What are you thinking?" he asked, glancing up and catching her off guard.

Her face heated but she held his gaze with an impish smile. "Just that you are a man of many talents, Mr. Roberts."

He brandished his butter knife like a sword. "You ain't seen nothing yet." He grinned and leaned over the counter to call up the stairs, "Girls, time to go," before slicing through the stack of sandwiches on the cutting board. "I made extra. They can have a drive-through breakfast for today. Next time, I won't burn the toast."

"Does that mean there will be a next time?" Grace's pulse skipped. *Did I really say that out loud?*

Kyle set the knife aside, wiped his hands on a

towel, and looked her in the eye as he strode to where she sat on a bar stool at the end of the counter. Cupping her cheek, he placed a tender kiss on her lips.

"I hope we have many nexts, Grace Donovan. You captivated me from the moment I saw you standing in the doorway of the gymnasium looking impossibly brave and beautiful. I haven't been able to get you out of my mind since. You're plucky, fearless and courageous, but you don't have to be strong all the time." He kissed her again, and this time the pressure of his mouth on hers made her heart soar. "I want to be a part of you and Cassie's lives, if you'll let me."

She wrapped her arms around him and buried her face in his neck, inhaling the musky scent. He was offering her the moon and the stars, and all she had was fear and stress to give in return. Was it selfish to take his gift and hold tight to the promise of companionship and maybe, in the future, a family?

She lifted her head and gazed at him, torn between the dream and her reality. "What about Avery? You know this study is no guarantee that Cassie will..." Her throat closed. Impossible to breathe the words she dreaded every waking hour.

Kyle nodded, his eyes grave. "Dr. Michaels is one of the best in his field, but there are others, Grace. If this process doesn't work, we'll keep trying. Don't shut us out. Avery will be fine. She's her father's child." He nuzzled her jaw. "So, is that a yes? Will you date the school principal at the risk of getting called teacher's pet?"

She smiled. "There are worse things they could call me. Yes, I would love to spend more quality time with you, Mr. Roberts. Just don't cook breakfast anymore, deal?"

"Hey! One mistake and a guy can never live it down. I'll have you know I make an award-winning quiche, just ask Avery." He stood and called the girls again. "Avery, Cassie. Get a move on, ladies. The bus leaves in five."

Instead of the expected stampede of noisy feet coming down the stairs, they were met with silence. The kind that sent chills up Grace's spine.

"Something is wrong," she whispered, rising to meet Kyle's suddenly grim gaze. "Why aren't they answering?"

"I don't know," he said, "But I'm going to find out." He squeezed her hand in reassurance, then strode out of the kitchen, his longer strides making it hard to keep up.

Grace followed, a myriad of nightmarish thoughts running through her mind. It wasn't like Cassie not to answer when called. Maybe they were in the upstairs bathroom getting ready and simply hadn't heard. *Let it be something like that and the girls were safe and sound —please.*

She'd taken two of the stairs up to the second floor behind Kyle when something made her look at the front foyer. Her stomach plunged. "Kyle, their coats aren't on the hooks. Our girls are gone."

KYLE WAS in the middle of searching Avery's bedroom and attached bathroom when Grace's cry froze him to the spot. Not in the house? That didn't make sense. Avery knew better than to go outside without asking first. They had a routine on school days, one that worked for both of them. Granted, today had been different, but still...

It didn't matter. He needed to find her, and then they'd have a father/daughter talk about breaking the rules.

Leaving her girly pink room, he charged down the short hall and lunged down the stairs to the entrance where Grace was feverishly trying to get bare feet into her boots.

"Where would they go? What if someone stole our babies?" Her face was sheet-white, her eyes frantic.

He took her arms and gave them a slight shake, shocking her into going still. "You need to calm down, honey. You won't do anyone any good going off in a panic. Now, do you have any idea where Cassie might go if she's upset?"

"Upset? Why would...?" Her eyes widened. "Oh. They heard us earlier, arguing. This is all my fault." Tears welled, but she brushed them away. "We're new to town. Cass has only made friends with a few kids. Avery, Thomas... Do you think they'd try to go to your brother's house? Didn't you say he lives nearby?"

Kyle swept her up in a quick heartfelt hug before bending to get his own shoes on. "You're a genius, my love. Avery adores her cousin. Rachel and Keith live two blocks over on Cedar Street, she knows the way. They'll be fine, Grace, don't worry." He reached for his jacket. "Stay here in case they come back. I'll call as soon as I find them—promise." He opened the door to drizzle, grimaced, and stepped onto the porch. "Those girls are grounded for life after this stunt."

Knowing he was stepping out of bounds but feeling parental frustration and worry for both kids, he let his ire out. Better now than after he tracked them down.

Giving a last reassuring wave to a woebegone Grace huddled on the porch, he turned to jog across his lawn, intending to take a shortcut to his brother's. It was a path he and Avery took often, so he had confidence she would do the same now, but just as he passed in front of the dripping sleigh, he heard a sound that was music to his ears.

Slipping on the wet grass, he slowed and moved to the cutout side of the sled. There, on the floor under protection of the front panel, Avery and Cassie sat bundled beneath the throw he hadn't removed from the sleigh ride. They had their heads under the blanket, and he could hear Avery reading her favorite holiday story, *The Night Before Christmas,* a book he'd passed onto her from his own childhood.

He glanced back at Grace and pointed to the sleigh with a thumbs up. She waved, her relief palpable. He knew two young ladies who were going to have a lot of chores to do in the next while. They'd scared a decade off his life with this stunt.

"See, Cass. Santa *can* perform miracles. He'll be able to make your mom happy again and save Daddy's job. We just have to wait here. When he comes to get the sleigh, we'll tell him we changed our minds and need a new Christmas wish. He'll do it, I know he will."

"But what if he doesn't come?" Cass asked in her timid voice. "Your dad said this is an extra sleigh. He might not even need it, and I'm cold. We should go back before we get in trouble."

Kyle smiled. At least one of them was practical. "I think it's too late for that, ladies." The blanket stilled, then two tousled heads poked out, each wearing identical expressions of dismay.

"Daddy—"

"Mr. Roberts—"

"We're sorry!" They jumped up and ran into his open arms.

"Girls, what were you thinking? Look at you, you're not even dressed." He shook his head at their foolhardiness and lifted them, one on each hip, out of the sleigh. "We'll talk about this inside. You'll be lucky if you don't catch a cold from this little misadventure."

The short hike up the hill to his house was a workout, but he refused to set them down now that he'd found them. His heart was still caterwauling in his chest, and fear had left a metallic tang in his mouth. The sudden insight into what Grace went through every time Cassie was admitted to the hospital left him humbled. He didn't know what he'd do if Avery ever got sick. Cope, there was no other choice.

Grace raced forward and took Cassie out of his arms as he climbed the stairs. She was crying again, but this time he figured it was relief coming through, not anger.

"They're okay," he reassured her as they reentered the house, the warmth a welcoming comfort on his chilled flesh. "Chastened and cold, but otherwise fine. Right, girls?"

"Yes, sir," they said in sync, their expressions woebegone now that the adventure was over and their punishment near.

Grace set Cass down and brushed trembling fingers over her damp hair. "Why would you go out in the rain like that? It's still dark, anything could have..." She swallowed hard, then reached out and pulled her child into her arms. "I love you more than the moon and stars. Please don't scare me like that again."

Cassie was blubbering now, too, her face buried in her mom's neck. "I won't, Mommy. I'm sorry. Me and Avery thought Santa Claus could come from the... the North Pole and change our wishes, so... so we waited in the sleigh, but he didn't come before Mr. Roberts came and now our wishes won't come true!" she ended on a wail.

"Oh, honey." Grace cuddled her girl and stared up at him with troubled eyes.

"Is this true, Avery?" Kyle dropped onto his haunches and took his daughter's hand, forcing her to meet his gaze. "You disobeyed rules and frightened Grace and I out of our minds because you wanted a different *gift*?" He couldn't believe what he was hearing. When did his little girl become so avaricious?

She solemnly nodded, her chin wobbling. "It wasn't just any gift though. We kind of overheard Mrs. Bigalow saying you could lose your job because you helped Ms. Donovan and I thought maybe Santa could give my puppy to someone else, so you could stay at Emerson Elementary, Daddy. All my friends are there, and I don't want to move like Cassie did."

Kyle shot Grace an apologetic glance before pulling his child in for a hug. "I appreciate you going to bat for me with Santa Claus, but next time, don't listen in on adult conversations, it's rude. I'm your father and I will do what is best for this family, understood?"

"Yes, Daddy." She straightened and looked at him with tearful eyes. "Am I still grounded?"

Looking at her sorrowful expression, his heart swelled with love. She may have done something wrong, but it was for the right reasons. How could he punish her for caring?

"We'll see. It'll depend on how fast you get up those stairs and dressed for school, young lady." He smiled to soften his words and patted her butt as she squealed and headed for her room. "And no running," he called, grinning as she made a concerted effort to climb with decorum—the little performer.

Grace released Cassie and eased back to see her face. "Is that why you ran away, too? Because Mrs. Bigalow said some rather unfortunate things?"

Kyle's smile faded. Tammy had taken her place in his life for granted. They'd been company for each other after their spouses left, but that's all. He'd made it clear from the onset he wasn't looking for a serious relationship—true, until Grace came along—and with her father's standing on the school board, it had made the entire situation between them all the more tenuous. He should have told her they were done. It might have saved them this morning's uncomfortable scene.

Cassie shrugged and dropped her gaze. "I couldn't let Avery go alone, especially after what Mr. Roberts did for us." Her big blue eyes found his and held on. "Do you believe in angels, Mr. Roberts?"

Floored, he could only nod, thinking maybe he did now.

"Me, too," she said, and ran over to kiss his cheek. "Can I go upstairs with Avery?"

Grace rose, looking as though she'd seen a ghost. "Yes, but no goofing around. Dress and get back down here. We really need to go."

"Okay," she agreed and trotted up the stairs with a cheery wave.

Kyle rose, too, his hand cradling his cheek as though he could hold the warmth inside. "Your daughter is a special little being."

Grace turned from the staircase, her eyes shining suspiciously wet. "Both girls are pretty great."

Yeah, they were.

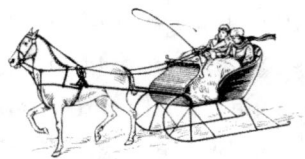

19

Emerson Elementary had pulled out all the stops for the holiday pageant. The gymnasium looked like a winter wonderland with the walls covered in paper snowflakes the kids had made in art class. A straggly tree sat in splendor on the right side of the stage, its limbs covered in popcorn garlands, painted picture cutouts, and candy canes. Chairs set in neat rows lined the floorspace below the stage, each one filled with smiling, clapping families there to support their loved ones.

Grace waited in the wings, her job for the evening to make sure the children knew their places and looked their best. Each class came out after an introduction given by Kyle, looking especially handsome in a steel-gray suit and maroon tie.

Some performed short, entertaining skits such as

the one Thomas, Kyle's nephew, did where he was the innkeeper who greeted the three wisemen the night baby Jesus was born. He'd worn a flowing robe that looked suspiciously like a gunnysack with a scarf wrapped around his waist and dark smudges on his cheeks and had spent half the play with his hand over his eyes trying to see past the lights to where his family sat in the crowded auditorium. At one point, a wiseman had to nudge him with his staff to remember his lines—so cute.

Now it was Cassie and Avery's turn. The girls were presenting a selection of songs with their music teacher. They looked adorable—if nervous—in matching black velvet dresses with white lace trim, white stockings, and patent leather shoes. Grace held her breath as they took their places high on one of the tiers that had been formed to look like a tree. Then the music started, and tears made it hard to see anything.

They had been through so much together, and her precious baby girl was thriving against the odds. She was overwhelmed and closed her eyes in gratitude. *"Your daughter is as smart and brave as you, my love. I think we're going to be okay."*

"Did you get any photos?" Kyle asked, slipping a hand around her waist as he joined her, his eyes shining.

Grace shook her head, smiling. "Not yet. Aren't they wonderful?"

Kyle sneaked a quick kiss and lifted the camera from around her neck. "They're acing it. I guess all the ear-blasting practice was worth it." He grinned and stepped forward to get a few shots. "Who knew twenty recorders could sound so good?"

They seemed like a Heavenly choir to Grace. She would never forget this night. Cassie would be starting her trial program in the new year, and while the prognosis was good, they'd learned to appreciate every moment for the gift it was.

Like now. Kyle came toward her. With the lights forming a halo around his head and the children's choir in the background, it took on a surreal quality as he wrapped her in his arms.

"Did I tell you how beautiful you look tonight?" He nuzzled her cheek.

"Yes, but I like hearing it," she murmured, tipping her head to the side to enjoy more of his caresses. "We shouldn't be doing this here. You're already on thin ice with the school board."

He gave her a last lingering kiss on the lips, then turned back to the kids. "The tree tier was a brilliant idea, thanks."

She sighed, missing his embrace already. "I saw it

on a television program and thought it was cute. I'm sorry, Kyle, I didn't mean to—"

He squeezed her hand. "No, you're right. I'm just happy, happier than I been in a long while, and it's because of you, Grace." He glanced down at her and grinned. "Even if you did talk me into getting a puppy."

She chuckled, while inside her heart glowed. "If I had to get one Mr., so did you. We're going to have two ecstatic girls this Christmas."

"That we are," he agreed, his gaze warm.

As they listened to the final song in the choir's program, Grace thought it was especially fitting—*We Wish You a Merry Christmas.*

A WORD ABOUT CHILDHOOD CANCER

Leukemia is the most common cancer in children and teens, accounting for almost 1 out of 3 cancers. Most childhood leukemias are acute lymphocytic leukemia (ALL). Most of the remaining cases are acute myeloid leukemia (AML). Chronic leukemias are rare in children.

Acute lymphoblastic leukemia (ALL) is most common in children 2 to 8 years old.

Kids with anemia may:

• look pale

• feel very tired, weak, or short of breath while playing

• bruise very easily, get a lot of nosebleeds, or bleed for a long time after even a minor cut

Other symptoms of leukemia can include:

• pain in the bones or joints, sometimes causing a limp

• swollen lymph nodes (swollen glands) in the neck, groin, or elsewhere

• poor appetite and weight loss

• fevers with no other symptoms

• belly pain

Sometimes leukemia can spread, or **metastasize**. If it spreads to the brain, symptoms may include headaches, seizures, balance problems, or vision problems. If it spreads to the lymph nodes in the chest, symptoms may include breathing problems and chest pain.

How Is Leukemia Treated?

A pediatric oncologist (a doctor who specializes in childhood cancer) will lead the medical team caring for a child with leukemia. The oncologist works with other specialists, including nurses, social workers, psychologists, and surgeons.

Chemotherapy is the main treatment for childhood leukemia. The dosages and drugs used may differ based on the child's age and the type of leukemia.

Other treatments include:

• radiation therapy: high-energy X-rays that kill cancer cells

• targeted therapy: specific drugs that find and attack cancer cells without hurting normal cells

Limited Institution Trials

Sometimes, clinical trials are performed in only a few hospitals. These are called Limited Institution Trials and they are able to answer a research question with fewer patients than most national trials require. Answers to important research questions can be obtained in a shorter time through such limited trials. COG limited institution trials are reviewed and approved in the same manner as all other clinical trials.

Pilot studies

Pilot studies are examples of limited institution trials. In these studies, investigators are studying a new treatment or therapy combination. Such studies are done at only a few institutions with a limited number of patients to see if the treatments are safe and effective against the targeted disease. If it is found to be effective, the new therapy may be open to more institutions. The results of pilot studies are compared to the best current treatments to find out if the new treatments are better in some way. Pilot studies also help to decide whether the drugs or therapies being tested should be investigated further using more patients.

If you or someone you know are affected by this cruel disease, here are some links that may help:

Sources:

Cancer.Org
Kids health.org
Healthline.com
Childrensoncology Group

PREVIEW THE SISTER PACT

Two sisters lose sight of what's most important- family bonds.

Holly Tremaine glared after the cabbie who'd just driven away with her carefully wrapped Christmas gifts in the backseat. She'd done everything short of flying to catch his attention, all to no avail. Now what was she going to do? She hadn't even caught the number of his taxi. The car was blue and white, and the cab driver had been an older man with pictures of his two grandchildren taped to his dash—that's all the information she had.

What a mess.

The bluebird of lost hopes—aka the cab—disappeared into the busy Victoria traffic leaving Holly alone to face her past. She swallowed hard and turned toward her parents' imposing two-story townhouse. The dismal day blended with the gray stone and black iron accents that had intimidated her as a child—nice to see some things remained the same.

Sighing, she tightened her grip on the carry-on bag she'd limited herself to for the flight—which is why she was now giftless—and trudged toward the big oak doors as though she were fighting her way through quicksand. Great. Not even in the house and she already regretted the trip.

The sign below the bell was no less glaring for the elegant script; No Soliciting, Fundraising, Salesmen, Religion or Politics- Thank you.

As though attaching manners at the end softened the cold tone the message conveyed. That was her parents in a nutshell.

She jabbed the bell like it was a release valve for her frustration. The rain that had held off while she dashed from store to store began to fall—a misty drizzle that sank into Holly's clothes and turned her hair lank in a matter of seconds. Wet and miserable, she waited for someone to let her in.

The door swung back revealing a yawning black maw—or so it seemed in that moment. The one person Holly had hoped to avoid stood in the entry.

Her sister.

"Holly." Susan looked down her slender, too perfect, nose. "You're late."

Holly blew a wayward strand of wet hair away from her face and tried to ignore the tic developing over her right eyebrow. "Well, I'm here now. Better late than never, right?" She glanced over her shoulder at the curtain of rain. "Mind letting me in? It's cold out here." She smiled and took a step forward, forcing her sister to move or get plowed down.

The grand entrance was just as inhospitable as she remembered. Dark wood climbed the walls while marble tile covered the floor like a layer of ice. Eight years and nothing had changed.

"Where are they?" she asked, though she knew the answer by glancing at her watch. Five o'clock, time for pre-dinner drinks in the lounge.

"Mom and Dad? Or Steven?"

The nervous tap-tapping of Susan's glossy black pump told Holly she wasn't nearly as calm as she pretended. For her part, Holly couldn't control the fluttering in her stomach at the thought of seeing Steven after all these years. Her sister looked... older—harder. Maybe married life hadn't turned out like she expected. Was it wrong Holly hoped that was true?

"I just arrived, Sue." They'd both used nicknames for each other as children. "Can we save the arguing until tomorrow? I'm beat."

Susan's expression softened as though she, too, regretted the distance that had grown between them. "Hols, we need to..."

"Who was at the door, darling? Your parents are acting even stranger than normal." Steven approached from down the hall, his view obstructed by his wife.

Breathe, Holly. She was going to hyperventilate and embarrass herself by passing out on the floor at their feet, she could see it now. Well, she could if not for the black dots dancing before her eyes. *Oh man*, he was every bit as striking as she remembered. Movie star handsome. And at one time, the love of her life. No matter how many pep-talks she'd given herself, nothing could have prepared her for this.

Her vision blurred. She leaned hard on the handle of her luggage as her knees wobbled, then gasped as the wheels slipped out from under her and she went down, landing hard on her elbow.

"Ow," she muttered, almost as an afterthought, too busy trying to control her flip-flopping tummy. "I don't feel so good." At least the tiles were cool on her back—small favors.

"Take it easy," a rich, deep voice murmured. And then he was there. Warm hands cradled her head while wide shoulders blocked the vision of Susan's surprisingly worried expression. Strange, she thought Susan would be laughing at her predicament.

"I'm fine," she snapped, wriggling to escape Steven's hold. But then she looked into his eyes and froze. Steven's eyes were the blue of a midnight sky. These eyes matched the winter storm lashing the window panes—grim and steely. "You," she whispered, stunned.

"Were you hoping for someone else?" Steven's annoying, pain-in-her-butt brother asked.

Holly lay back and closed her eyes. "Why can't I catch a break?"

Get your copy here

AFTERWORD

Reviews are the lifeblood of any successful author. Without you, we can't be heard. If you enjoy the story, please consider sharing on your favorite social media sites:

Please click here to post a review:

Amazon

BookBub

Goodreads

Thank you,

Jacquie Biggar

MY GIFT TO YOU!

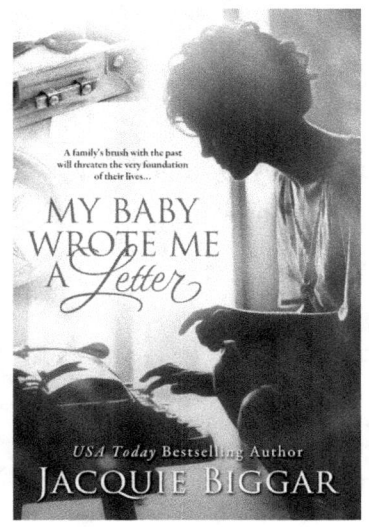

My Baby Wrote Me A Letter

A family's brush with the past will threaten the fabric of their lives.

Eight months pregnant and her Navy husband away on a mission, Grace Freeman craves the security of her childhood home in Canada.

When a letter written by her long-lost mother is found in an old writing desk it creates a tear in the fabric of her family.

Can Grace find a way to bring peace to those she loves, or will a message from the past destroy their future?

Newsletter subscribers also get bonus content and insider information every month. I love giveaways and there is lots of interesting stuff for me to share with you!

Newsletter- Sign up Now!

ABOUT THE AUTHOR

Jacquie Biggar is a USA Today bestselling author of romance who loves to write about tough, alpha males and strong, contemporary women willing to show their men that true power comes from love. She lives on Vancouver Island with her husband and loves to hear from readers all over the world!

In her own words:

"My name is Jacquie Biggar. When I'm not acting like a total klutz I am a wife, mother of one, grandmother, and a butler to my calico cat.

My guilty pleasures are reality tv shows like Amazing Race and The Voice. I can be found every Monday night in my armchair plastered to the television laughing at Blake's shenanigans.

I love to hang at the beach with DH (darling hubby) taking pictures or reading romance novels (what else?).

I have a slight Tim Hortons obsession, enjoy gardening, everything pink and talking to my friends."

Subscribe to her Newsletter and follow her on these sites:

Amazon | Website | Facebook | Newsletter
Twitter | Pinterest | GoodReads | Bookbub

ALSO BY JACQUIE BIGGAR

Wounded Hearts Series

Tidal Falls

The Rebel's Redemption

Twilight's Encore

The Sheriff Meets His Match

Summer Lovin'

Wounded Hearts Box Set

Maggie's Revenge

With This Heart

The SEAL's Temptation

Secrets, Lies & Alibis

Mended Souls Series

The Guardian

The Beast Within

Virtually Gone

Gambling Hearts

Hold 'Em

Crazy Little Thing Called Love

My Girl

Married to The Texan- Box set

Blue Haven

Sweetheart Cove

Sunset Beach

Men of WarHawks

Skating on Thin Ice

The Player

Single Titles

Silver Bells

The Lady Said No

My Baby Wrote Me A Letter

Tempted by Mr. Wrong

Valentine: A Hearts and Kisses Romance

Mistletoe Inn

The Sister Pact

Perfectly Imperfect

Love, Me